Sea Change

Book Two of Devi Jones' Locker

Darusha Wehm

Sea Change
Book Two of Devi Jones' Locker
by Darusha Wehm

Published by *in potentia* press

cover illustration © NatuskaDPI

ISBN 978-0-9941332-3-6

Devi Jones' Locker:

Packet Trade
Sea Change
Storm Cloud (coming soon)

Science Fiction by M. Darusha Wehm

Beautiful Red
Children of Arkadia

Andersson Dexter novels:

Self Made
Act of Will
The Beauty of Our Weapons

Chapter One

Fair Winds and Following Seas

The island slowly shrank as we sailed away. I couldn't see anything happening when I looked right at it, but when I went down below for a while, then came back, it was shocking to see how far we'd come. It was unnerving to watch something disappear incrementally.

I'd only spent a few days at Isla Isabela, but I couldn't shake the feeling that I was leaving home. I'd come to know my way around the place; I knew the best route to get from the lagoon to town on foot, I knew which grocery store carried the good cheese, I had a favourite restaurant. And I already missed the bakery that made raisin bread in old coffee cans so it came out as a ridged cylinder.

I was nostalgic for a place I'd only visited, but it was just a way of covering up my nervousness. The longest ocean passage I'd ever been on was four days and that had seemed monumental at the time. Now I knew the *Byte Bucket* would be at sea for weeks, possibly close to to a month, of total isolation. I wasn't afraid, exactly — I trusted the captain and the rest of the crew completely, and they'd demonstrated that they knew what they were doing — but it was daunting nonetheless. So I focussed on the island and tried to see it recede into the distance of space and time.

Jim "Call Me Jimmy" Houghton, ship's cook and resident old salt popped his head out of the companionway. "Anyone mind if I load up the tunes?"

Heads shook and the captain said, "Go for it." Jimmy disappeared and a few seconds later the opening notes of "Rock the Casbah" boomed out of speakers cleverly built into the sides of the bench seats in the cockpit. Mat, the captain, grinned at me. "We don't stand on ceremony much on this boat, but the first day at sea is usually a dance party night."

I frowned. "We didn't do this on our last passage."

Mat tossed her head, dreadlocks swaying. "We didn't want to spook you. Besides, that was only a couple of days. This is the real thing. We ought to celebrate. Come on, Devi, let's dance!" With that, she grabbed my hand and began to dance around the cockpit. The other crew members joined us, filling the spacious area. Tulia and Martin, the two junior sailors, danced nearby but not together in that tried and true method of high-schoolers who like each other. They were pretending that there was nothing between them, but we all knew better. I grinned at Martin and watched him blush and avoid my eyes. Tulia had been jealous of my friendship with him at first, but after she found out about my ex-girlfriend, she'd warmed up to me. And here I'd been worried that she'd be nervous about sharing a bunk room with a queer girl.

Mat and I shared an incredulous look as Jimmy appeared out of nowhere and tried to get a mosh going with Christine, the mechanic, and the mate, Isaac. They were probably half his age, but at times you'd never know it.

It was a better ride than I'd been expecting. The wind wasn't very strong and we were on what I'd learned was called a beam reach — where the wind is blowing over the side of the boat. Isaac, the ship's mate, had told me that it was the fastest point of sail, though it could often be uncomfortable because the ocean waves hit the boat broadside. However, today we were lucky — the swell was astern even though the wind was abeam; a perfect sail.

"Fair winds and following seas," I said, echoing the phrase I'd heard sailors say when they wished each other well.

"Enjoy it while it lasts," Mat said, twirling around with her arms in the air. "The one truth about the weather is that it will change."

⚓

The dance party didn't last long; only a couple more songs, then Jimmy went down to work on dinner and the crew settled into their routine. I tried to decide what to do with myself since my place on the boat when we were under way was still a bit ambiguous. *Byte Bucket* wasn't just a sailboat, it was also the home of one of the nodes for the bizarre cloud data storage firm *Really Remote Desktop*, and that was why I was there. This hundred-foot sloop was my co-op job placement as part of my Computer Science degree. The server room built into the bilge was my domain, but when we were sailing my job was to stay out of the way and make sure I didn't fall overboard.

I made my way out of the cockpit and into the main salon that was built up in front of the working end of the boat. It was a large open space with a lovely hardwood floor that was much better suited to a dance party than the cockpit, but there was something about hanging out in the cockpit at sea that just felt right. Open air, the sound of the waves — it was where you wanted to be when you were getting underway.

Inside, there was a TV and a bar, plus seating along the sides, so we spent more time here in bad weather or when we were trying to just relax out of everyone else's way. No one was there now as I made my way to the interior of the boat by hanging on to the evenly spaced handholds along the wall. It was almost second nature now, but I still had the odd bruise from my first few days on board.

I carefully stepped down the companionway stairs facing backwards. They were steep and while most of the crew walked down them facing forward, I wasn't keen on ending up on my butt. Down below was taken up with the galley on one side with its kitchen area and large table where we shared meals. There was a short hallway with toilets and showers along the sides, which led to the shared bunk room. That was where I ran into Martin.

"No regrets?"

He made a face. "What would be the point? I can't exactly change my mind now." I'd been sure he was going home when we were in the Galápagos. I didn't know the details of his contract, but I knew he'd only signed on in a desperate bid to earn enough money to get back home after getting stranded in Mexico. I could understand the tension between wanting to get home and the call of adventure. Especially if adventure wasn't exactly what you were looking for.

I nodded. There wasn't any reason to belabour it — if he wished he'd made a different choice, it was too late now. "You going to check on the servers?"

"Might as well," I said. "I should get into the habit of monitoring them daily. I'm kind of hoping I can figure out some way to get a little speed boost out of them. I know that the transfer rates I'm seeing are consistent with this application, but it's just so hard to accept when you're used to proper broadband..." Martin looked like I felt when the others got deep into the boat talk. "Sorry. I guess I'm just rubber ducking."

"You what?"

I laughed. "It's programmer-speak for thinking out loud. It's not about conversation — you could be talking to a rubber duck."

"Well, I'd like to think I'm more useful than bath toy, but it wouldn't be true in this conversation."

"I'll try to keep my more boring conversations to myself."

"Nah, I don't mind being your rubber duck," Martin said, "so long as you don't expect anything more complex than *quack* in response."

We were both laughing when Tulia came around the bulkhead. "What are you two up to? That sounded kinda dirty," she said, grinning.

"It's — not," I said, still laughing. "I was going on about work and then I said I was—"

"Never mind," Martin interrupted. "It's too hard to explain."

Tulia rolled her eyes at us but she was smiling. "I'm on night watch tonight, so I'm going to try to get a nap in. I hope this *rubber ducking* isn't too loud."

"Oh, god," Martin said as she carefully walked down the passage toward the bunks, her round body jiggling as she laughed. I noticed him following her with his eyes and hid a smirk. "That did sound pretty bad."

"Could have been worse. I could have been explaining about the interaction between the master and the slave."

"I had no idea you computer nerds were so kinky."

"Seriously?" I asked. "You *have* been on the internet, right?" He made a face and I chucked him on the shoulder. "I'm heading down to my dungeon. See you at dinner?"

"Yeah, if I don't get bored and come down to spy on your arcane rituals first."

⚓

Data in, data out. I'd always found watching the pattern of data flow relaxing. Once you knew what to look for you could kind of get a sense of what it was. Not specifically, of course, but between file size and transfer rate you could make an educated guess — a high res movie, downloaded from somewhere nearby; a bunch of image files, from a server further away; an album of mp3s, from someone on dial-up. It wasn't so clear on the *Bucket*, since mostly we were our own bandwidth bottleneck. But I watched while a couple of movie-size files moved around and many small uploads occurred — probably desktop backups of documents.

It reminded me of pictures taken from orbit I'd seen of the Earth at night. The patterns of lights could tell a kind of story — about where there was activity, and when. Metadata, the story about the story. I liked that kind of thing.

If I hadn't been mesmerized by the packets, I probably wouldn't have been able to pinpoint the time it happened, but I was watching the normal peaks and valleys when, very right before my eyes, the transfer rate spiked. And it stayed up; much higher than I'd seen it before on these servers. I was pretty sure the system could handle it, but it was odd, so I pulled up the logs. There was a clear increase, but not from a single user like I'd expected. The connections were coming from all over.

I frowned. It wasn't a typically alarming amount of traffic — certainly on a normal, contemporary database this wouldn't even rate as unusual. But for us... Could it be the start of a DDoS?

A distributed denial-of-service attack was a standard black hat hacker's tool for causing mischief and mayhem. Using many machines, usually the personal computers of innocent victims of malware, the attackers flooded the target with the goal of crippling their resources by overwhelming their bandwidth. Our entire business model relied on our servers being accessible to our clients — if we were down, we were losing business. Being bandwidth-challenged, we were particularly vulnerable to this kind of attack, though our distributed server network was designed to help mitigate that possibility. I wished I knew what was going on at the other server nodes.

In my orientation I'd been told that I was expected to work independently. The strength of RRD's system was that each set of servers ran as if it were the only one; we were all each other's failsafes. When my node was down, the others covered. If it were a deliberate attack, and each of us were overwhelmed, well, that was the point of a DDoS. Knowing whether it was happening all over didn't really change my course of action, I just wanted to know.

That got me thinking. I looked at the data transfer graph for the last hour. The spike was obvious and it had plateaued now, which was somewhat good news. I did a little mental math — with four nodes operating at an average of n, if one failed then we'd each have an increase of roughly $.25n$. Not enough to account for the more than doubling I was seeing. But if they'd all failed...

I made a decision. I sent a short email to headquarters describing the spike, making it clear that I had it under control for now, but that it was concerning. I'd rather catch hell for being overcautious than let the whole enchilada go bad because I didn't want to bother anyone.

I watched a while longer, but the traffic was stable. There wasn't anything I could do unless things changed, so I figured I might as well go back above decks and check out the view. Hopefully the open ocean would take my mind off it for a while.

⚓

I'd missed the shift changeover from day to night and when I got up to the cockpit the night shift crew were subdued as usual. I looked out to sea as the sunset painted the sky a vivid red.

"Sailors' delight," Jimmy said, his hand on the windward lifeline. He turned to me. "Hungry?"

"Yeah," I answered, only now realizing that it was true. He pointed me toward a tray of cheese, fish, and cut veggies.

"Get it while it's good," he said. "There won't be fresh stuff much longer."

I made up a plate for myself and, careful to staying out of Issac's way as he stood at the wheel, found my usual corner to wedge into. I watched the swell come up behind us, lifting the stern as it rolled underneath us. It was still an odd sensation, such a large and solid thing as the boat being tossed around like a cork.

"Cat got your tongue?" Tulia said, sliding in next to me. I shook my head. "Everything okay?" she asked, the smile on her face dissolving into a concerned look.

I nodded. "Yeah. Well, no, but it's just the servers. I'm fine."

"Okay." She didn't look convinced, but she didn't

press it. "It can get weird out here; the solitude and insignificance. Don't feel like you have to keep it to yourself if it starts getting to you."

"Thanks, I think." I made a face. "I wasn't worried before, but now..." I grinned to let her know I was kidding.

She nodded but her frown didn't disappear. "You get a lot of time to think out here. Maybe too much. It's easy to get caught up in what's to come, what might be..." She was staring out to sea with such an intensity that I looked to see what she was looking at. But there was only ocean and sky, illuminated by the sinking sun. "It's easy to replay conversations, dwell on mistakes. There's nothing to distract you. It can sometimes be hard to remember to enjoy the moment."

Had something happened between her and Martin? It sounded like she was talking to herself more than to me, but it didn't feel right to ask. She had a point, though. Was I so bothered by the strange server traffic because it was so unusual, or was it just that I couldn't find out about the other servers? I'd never worked in such isolation before. Even when I'd had individual projects, I could at least look things up online, talk to people who had experience with similar issues. Now I was on my own, and I wondered if I were just getting lost in my own head.

And it was only our first day at sea.

Chapter Two

Controlled Chaos

I sat in the cockpit until well after dark, watching the reflection of the stars on the water. I could see why some of the crew didn't like night watch — you couldn't see much, and I'm sure the night was long — but I found it beautiful. It had been a long day, though, and I could feel the gravity of my eyelids. I could have slept in the cockpit if I'd wanted, but my bunk was closer to a real bed. I said goodnight to Tulia and Isaac, then made my careful way down below.

I stopped off in the server room and popped open the laptop. It took a moment to connect the email client, and I stared at the unchanging inbox for several minutes. I double checked the connection and asked for new mail a couple of times, but there wasn't any answer to my question to headquarters. I checked the logs and traffic was still high, but not beyond the capabilities of the system. Nothing had changed.

I reluctantly closed down the laptop and headed for my bunk. There wasn't actually a problem, not now, and there wasn't anything for me to do. But I sure didn't like the silence from headquarters. I lay in my narrow bunk, held in by the bulkhead on one side and a heavy curtain on the other which ran the length of my berth, offering privacy as well as security. The rhythmic rolling of the boat in the swells rocked me from side to side, its motion somehow simultaneously comforting and disconcerting.

I'd been sure I would drop off to sleep immediately, but now that I was in bed I was wide awake.

It can get weird out here... Tulia's concern echoed in my mind as I stared into the darkness of my small bunk. It seemed impossible, but I'd been aboard for only two weeks. It felt a lot longer. But only a few weeks ago I'd been playing X-Box with Nico and Jeannette. A wave of sadness washed over me. I missed my brother, Nico, and my parents, but they weren't the ones I was thinking about now.

When I closed my eyes, I couldn't help but remember the way the corners of her eyes crinkled when she laughed, the little curl of hair by her ear that would never stay put in a ponytail. Her painted toenails. The feeling of her fingers entwined with mine.

The scientist part of me understood why Jeannette had broken up with me. Our relationship wasn't that serious; it wasn't strong enough to justify turning down this opportunity and it wouldn't have survived the separation. But I also knew that if I'd gotten a different job for my work experience, I'd be sleeping curled up next to Jeannette right now instead of trying to figure out how to get comfortable in this tiny bunk. It wasn't fair.

⚓

I couldn't tell how long the sun had been up when I rolled out of bed, but the day was in full swing when I made it up to the cockpit. Martin and Christine were tweaking the sails while the captain eyed their handiwork, a battered paperback with a generic topless man on the cover in her lap.

"Morning," she said to me, then to the crew, "That's good there." Martin and Christine tidied up the bitter ends of the lines they'd been handling then came back to the aft of the cockpit. I looked around and was struck by the limitlessness of the sea. The ocean and the sky were only slightly different shades of the same hue and it was like being in the middle of an infinite sphere. I had a moment of vertigo, but it passed as movement on the ship caught my attention. It was Martin settling down into a corner of the cockpit, an open notebook and pen in his hands.

I'd never been seen the appeal of keeping a journal, but there was no doubt that our situation lent itself to introspection. I thought that days at sea would involve near-constant card games and conversations, but we all gravitated to solitary pursuits. There was some social time, of course — meals, impromptu events like the previous night's dance party, but the real isolation of being the only humans within visual range made us all more inclined to solitude.

Thinking of meals made my stomach growl. Looking around it became apparent that I'd missed breakfast, but there was always coffee on in the galley. Even if Jimmy wasn't around I could find something to eat, so I made my way down to the mess area located under the main salon. There was a jug of stuff that looked like milk in the chest refrigerator built onto the counter — reconstituted from powder, probably. I added a splash to my coffee and grimaced at the odd taste. I shook a little sugar in, which did wonders, then I grabbed some bread and jam.

I ate alone at the long table near the galley, not trusting myself to be able to carry it all up to the cockpit without dropping something or falling over. The coffee was helping, but I was still groggy from a poor night's sleep. After I'd finally dropped off, I kept waking up from the movement of the boat. It wasn't bad, but I wasn't used to it yet. On our previous passage from Costa Rica to the Galápagos I'd eventually gotten accustomed to sleeping aboard, but I felt like I spent most of the passage tired. I didn't think I'd be able to manage nearly a month of that feeling. Already I was worried about my ability to make good decisions.

I finished eating and poured another cup of coffee, finding the matching lid for my cup, then went down to the server room. It was accessible only from a vertical ladder, and it was slow going with my full cup. The boat wasn't rolling much, but I knew that it would be better if I unlatched the laptop desk. It was an all-in-one workstation with a built-in seat that was cleverly hinged. When it wasn't latched, it swung freely, keeping everything in the station, including me, more or less stable regardless of the movement of the boat. I climbed in and booted up the laptop.

Still no word from headquarters and traffic was up even more today. I worried my bottom lip between my teeth, running a few calculations. Our servers were handling it and the increase was gradual and natural-looking. If this was an attack, it wasn't a very effective one. But the numbers were clear — if the traffic kept increasing at this rate, we'd be overloaded well before we made landfall. And being cut off from the rest of the servers, there wouldn't be anything I could do about it.

⚓

I spent the rest of the morning reading and trying not to come up with reasons why headquarters hadn't answered my email. It wasn't working.

The most likely scenario was that I'd failed to send it somehow. Our system was strange enough that it was possible. Or maybe they were just busy and hadn't gotten around to it. Was it the weekend? A public holiday? I'd lost track of the calendar already. I put down my paperback and booted my phone. It turned out to be a Tuesday. How could I have so completely lost track of something as simple as the day of the week? I turned my phone back off to conserve its battery and picked up my book again. I stared at the page and thought about more implausible scenarios.

I was so lost in my head that I didn't hear Tulia come into the room.

"Good book?" She had a funny look on her face.

"It's all right," I said. She laughed and picked it out of my hands. It was upside down.

"Really?"

"It's this stupid server thing," I said, feeling like an

idiot. "I haven't heard anything from the office and I just can't stop wondering what's going on out there."

She nodded and sat down next to me. "Being cut off from the rest of the world takes some getting used to. You just have to accept that things happen in their own time and if there's an issue you'll just have to deal with it later. Of course, that's a lot easier said that done, am I right?"

"Yeah. I don't—" My thought was cut off by an enormous crashing sound from the deck in front of us and, almost simultaneously, the boat leaning over sharply. Isaac's head popped in through the open hatch.

"Both of you, on deck, now."

I looked at Tulia, hoping for an indication of what was happening and why I was being summoned, too, but she was already on her way out.

My heart hammered in my chest. I grabbed my inflatable personal floatation device from the shelf near the hatchway to the deck and shrugged it on.

When I got out I couldn't figure out what I was seeing. Almost everyone was on deck, a balloon of brightly coloured material poured like liquid all over the front of the deck, spilling over the low side of the sharply leaned over boat.

"Clip in," Isaac said, "then grab and haul." I looked down at the climbing-grade carabiner attached to a tether on the front of my PFD. There was a wire running the length of the deck and I saw that the others had all attached their tethers to the line. I fumbled with the catch and eventually got it secured, then took hold of the material nearest to where I was standing. It took a second before I realized that our sail was overboard. How were we even still upright?

I started to pull it aboard, shocked at how difficult it was. We were all hauling it in, but it was like we were pulling it up from the bottom of the sea. It felt like we weren't making any headway, and I was having a hard time breathing. I could sense that I was starting to panic; all I could think of was the weight of the sail in the water pulling us over. It seemed to take forever, but eventually I heard a shout from the bow. "Got the head!"

Martin had reached the edge of the sail and Isaac and Christine moved over to join him as they pulled up the rest of the huge sodden sail. The boat's trim evened out quickly as the sail came up on to the deck and soon we were back to normal — if hardly moving at all through the water.

Once the sail was on deck Isaac told Martin, "Get back to the cockpit and pull out the genny." Martin quickly moved aft and in a flurry of pulling on lines and grinding of winches had the large foresail out in record time. Immediately we picked up speed again. I just tried to stay out of the way and calm down. I didn't know how dangerous that had really been, but it was the first time since I came aboard that something had gone really wrong. The analytical part of my mind was impressed with how seamlessly everyone had worked together, but my lizard brain was still freaking out. What the hell had happened?

"Devi, you okay?" Isaac's voice startled me and I nodded, though that was probably a lie. "Can you help us stretch this out on deck?"

I nodded again and picked my way over to the soaking mess that was the sail. We each took an edge, then pulled it out as much as possible, laying the wet material over all the fixtures and fittings on the deck. It was hard to move at first, but once we got it stretched out it wasn't that bad. Isaac came around with random objects to weigh it down, then began to inspect the sail.

"What happened?" Tulia finally asked the question which had been occupying my thoughts.

"I'm not sure," Isaac said, scrutinizing one of the points of the sail. "We were sailing full and by, when all of a sudden the chute was in the drink." He picked around on the deck for a moment, then looked at something in his palm.

"Aha. The shackle snapped." He held out the piece of offending metal.

"Shit," Tulia said. "Rusted?"

Isaac shook his head. "Looks fine — just faulty, I guess. I hate when that happens." He pocketed the broken fitting. "We'll try to let this dry out before we bag it. We'll have to check for tears when we do, too."

Tulia nodded then asked, "Anything else for now?"

"Naw," Isaac said, "you're free." She nodded and headed back down below. He turned to me. "Thanks for the help, Devi. And sorry for being so abrupt with you — sometime we just have to do first and explain later, you know?"

"Yeah," I said. "It's okay. I'm glad I was useful." Issac nodded once then went back to the sail. I didn't move and was started by a voice behind me.

"Freaked out?" It was Christine.

I nodded, embarrassed, but what could I do? I *was* freaked out.

"Well, get over it. It's not like we were ever in any real danger. It takes more than a sail overboard to capsize a boat like the *Bucket*."

"But the shackle," I said. "Does stuff just break like that?"

"Of course," she said. "Everything breaks eventually. That's why we have a whole locker full of spares. And why we have a crew. I know they don't teach this stuff at university, but failure is part of the process. That's why they say that long-distance sailing is just fixing your boat in exotic locations, though I suppose you've never heard that either." She walked off, shaking her head as if my reaction were ludicrous.

Her attitude didn't do much for me, but her explanation did make me feel a little better. And now that I thought of it, the crew had acted as if this were an expected, if unusual, part of their work.

I carefully picked my way back to the cockpit. I felt as unsteady on my feet as I had the first day I stepped aboard.

⚓

I thought I'd put the morning's excitement behind me.

When Martin told me that it was good luck the sail hadn't been damaged, at first I didn't even know what he was talking about. I made some headway on my paperback and watched the ocean slip by. It didn't even occur to me to check the email for a message from headquarters. That was a sure sign that something was wrong.

We were all together in the cockpit for dinner, and the broken shackle was old news by nightfall. Mat talked with Isaac about the weather forecast she'd downloaded off the satellite while the rest of us kept our own councils. The mood was subdued, but not unusual enough to cause concern.

The sun went down and the day watch went down below. "Enjoying the night sky?" Martin asked as he passed me on the way to the bunks.

"Yeah." I looked up at the chunk of moon poking out from one of the few clouds. "I'll be down in a bit."

I made out a nod in the moonlight as he turned back to head into the boat. I wasn't really out here to look at the stars. I thought I had been, but as the darkness filled in it hit me. I was scared something else would happen. Every little noise made me think something was breaking. When I was down below all I could do was imagine catastrophe after catastrophe on deck. It was ridiculous. It wasn't like I could do anything about it even if there were a problem, and I knew full well the crew could handle it. I just couldn't deal with not knowing what was going on.

"You joining the night watch?" Mat asked, a smile

on her face.

"Maybe." I sighed. "I'm having a little trouble getting into the rhythm, I guess. I'm so tired, but..."

"You have to try and get some rest. Tired people make dumb decisions and that's how problems happen."

"Is that what happened this morning?" I asked without thinking, then immediately regretted it. "Sorry — I didn't mean to accuse anyone of anything..."

Mat shook her head, nonplussed. "This morning was just bad luck. Shit happens, things break, that's just reality. But how we respond to it when shit happens, that's where the good decisions and bad decisions matter. A lot of what we do out here is reacting to stuff we can't control. Sure, I plot our course, read the weather and plan accordingly, but even the best forecast is inaccurate. All you can do is make the best decision you can based on the information you have, then be able to adapt as necessary when the conditions turn out to be something completely different."

"How can you do that?" I asked. "How can you plan for something you won't know will happen?"

"People do that all the time, it's just a bit more obvious out here. Think about it: your car breaks down, a water pipe bursts, you get an unexpected visitor — life is always chaotic. All any of us can ever do is try to be as prepared as we can be and create conditions that minimize the chances of something going really wrong."

"That's not very reassuring."

Mat laughed as if I'd said something genuinely

hilarious. "Try to get some sleep," she said. "Don't make me pull rank."

"Okay." I went down below and climbed into my bunk. I stared up at the ceiling, imagining giant waves battering the hull, tornadoes driving the sea into a tempest, lightning storms striking the mast.

Life is always chaotic. Well, sure. But isn't the point to try and make it orderly?

Violent rocking jolted me awake. At first I had a moment of panic when I couldn't figure out how to get out of my bunk. Tiredness never did much for my ability to reason and the fact that my environment was shifting around me didn't help. However, I needed to know what was going on and I wasn't going to be able to figure that out down below.

I extricated myself from my bunk and made my way up above decks. I was surprised to find another bright, sunny tropical day, the sky a cloudless blue. If I didn't look at the sea, I'd have wondered if I were imagining the pitching and rolling of the boat.

I clung to a handhold by the companionway and looked aft. The ocean looked like a mountain range as seen from above, the peaks of the waves frothing like the top of an ice cream float. They weren't breaking like surf waves; if they had been it would have looked like that old Japanese painting of the Giant Wave you see everywhere. My stomach dropped as one of them rolled under us, a little off to the side — the boat picked up and it felt like the whole world was tilted over. We levelled off as the wave slid under us, but I could see that it was a never-ending roller coaster.

"It got a little rough overnight." Christine hung onto doorway as she came into the main salon then flopped down on to the seat. She unsnapped her PFD and let it drop to the floor. "Man, that's tiring. Just sitting around reading a book is like doing a set of abdominal crunches." She rubbed her stomach as punctuation.

"Is this..." I waved my hands in the general direction of the stern, but I meant everything, "is this okay?"

Christine rolled her eyes. "Obviously, it's not dangerous or anything. The boat's fine." She looked at me and I saw something in her face change. Her voice softened a little and she stopped looking at me like I was just in her way. Maybe she felt sorry for me. "It is uncomfortable as hell, though. It's impossible to relax when we're rolling like this." As if to underscore her point, a particularly large wave came through, throwing me into Christine's lap.

"Sorry," I said, sliding off her and grabbing something to hang on to. She didn't seem to notice my embarrassed flush, at least.

"Fuck, I hate this," she said, a scowl crossing her face. "Mat says it should chill out in a day or two, but I hope it's sooner. This is the worst. I can't even get a decent stretch in, let alone a whole routine."

Christine usually practiced yoga daily, and it hadn't occurred to me how hard that must be when the boat was moving like this. I had an idea.

"Hey," I said. "Is there stuff you can do while seated? Like, in a chair?"

She shrugged. "Sure. But it's too rough even for that."

I shook my head. "I don't mean here. Why not go to the server room? My workstation down there is gimballed. It probably won't be great, but you might at least be able to relax a little."

"Really? That would be—" A look of what I can only describe as intense longing crossed her face. "That would be so good. Is it okay if I try it out now?" I nodded. "Thanks, Devi. I owe you one." She grabbed her discarded PFD and staggered down the companionway.

I looked out to the cockpit. Mat and Martin were hunkered down on either side of the wheel, wedged as well as possible into their seats, but I could see what Christine meant about the constant sit-ups. They were both just sitting there, but they had to work to stay in place. Mat seemed reasonably content with the situation, but Martin's face showed plainly that he wished he were anywhere but here.

I just managed to grab on to the nearby handhold before I was thrown off the seat. It was miserable. I should have been hungry, but the thought of food turned my stomach. I was tired, I couldn't work with Christine using my workstation anyway — screw it. I went back to bed.

⚓

Conditions were still rough when I woke, desperate to pee. I had to hang on just to go to the toilet and for the first time I was grateful that the bathroom was so small. The incongruous thought came to me that this was probably what it was like for astronauts in outer space, having to constantly hold on to something while they did the most ordinary activities. That made the situation seem a lot cooler; at least, until I was thrown into the wall when I tried to pull up my pants. I understood now why I was told to always pump the toilet until it was dry. That could have been really gross.

I banged my way out of the head and set out for the galley. I still felt a bit unwell, but it had probably been twelve hours since I'd eaten. I saw Jimmy through the serving hatch and I was amazed at the easy way he worked. He wasn't even hanging on to anything.

"Morning," he said, noticing me.

"Is is still morning?"

He nodded. "You missed breakfast, though. Lunch won't be up for an hour or so — how about a ginger snap?"

"You're brilliant!" I took the pair of small cookies he offered and slid into a seat. I nibbled on one, and it appeared to agree with me, so I gobbled down the rest of it. The other one disappeared shortly thereafter.

"How do you do it?" I asked, watching him prepare lunch. "Is it just practice?"

"Is what just practice?"

"Being able to stand there, no hands, while the boat's rocking and rolling like this."

He looks confused for a moment, then laughed, his long gray ponytail swaying along with the movement of the boat. "Oh, Devi. There's no trick to it. Come in here and I'll show you."

I carefully made my way over to the door to the

galley and looked in. Jimmy was effectively tied to the counter by a heavy strap slung behind him and pulled snugly tight. He couldn't have fallen over if he'd tried. I don't know why it was so surprising — in hindsight, the idea of strapping in was obvious — but it was like being slapped in the face by a wave. I must have been standing there with my mouth hanging open, because Jimmy stared at me with a half-amused, half-concerned look on his face.

"You need to get it together, Devi. It's easy to get off-kilter on a passage — not enough sleep, not enough food... when was the last time you drank some water?"

"I dunno—" I started to say when the floor came out from under me. It was like everything happened simultaneously and in slow motion; I heard a crash, felt myself falling, saw the edge of the counter across from Jimmy and knew I was going to hit it, hard. It seemed like more than enough time passed to be able to do something — grab a handhold, twist out of the way — but it was like watching a scary movie where you can see the monster coming up behind the people, but you can't warn them. I was paralyzed. I felt the impact but nothing really hurt... until I turned.

It was like someone was stabbing me in the side. I stopped moving and breathed shallowly.

"Oh, shit." Jimmy unclipped himself and knelt down next to me. He gently prodded at my ribs. For a moment I thought it was okay, then he hit the spot. I yelped and he moved back quickly.

"You've busted a rib," he said. "Bruised, broken, I

don't know but it doesn't really matter anyway. There's nothing we can do for it except tape you up to stop you moving too much and wait for it to get better."

Tears were pricking the back of my eyes, even though I'd wedged myself into a position where it didn't hurt. How could I have been so dumb? I knew it was rough, why wasn't I holding on to something?

"I'm sorry," I said, trying to keep control of my voice.

"It happens," Jimmy said, his face softening. "Especially when you're tired. But you haven't made things any easier on yourself, that's for sure." He left to go get help, which was good because I didn't really want him to see me cry but I couldn't hold it back anymore.

⚓

Tulia was in her pajamas — hot pink boxers and a matching tank top — and blinking the sleep from her eyes. I felt even worse knowing that Jimmy had gotten her up to deal with me. I was so stupid. My throat closed up again but I bit the inside of my cheek until the threat of tears passed.

"You're lucky you didn't bang your head." She looked at Jimmy sharply. "She didn't…"

He shook his head. "I saw it." He jerked his head in the direction of the counter's corner. "Cracked her ribs right over there."

Tulia's face softened and she knelt down to where I still lay carefully not moving. "We're going to have to sit you up and get your top off." She looked up at Jimmy and didn't say anything, but he understood and wandered off somewhere else. "You wearing a bra?"

I shook my head, wincing at the movement. She nodded and helped me slowly work myself into a sitting position. I made it up with only one stab and a gasp, then got myself wedged against the cupboard.

"Lifting your arms is probably going to hurt."

"Okay."

It felt like forever as we wrestled my shirt up and off, but pretty soon I was sitting there topless while Tulia fussed with a roll of athletic tape. She wrapped it around me tightly, while I held my breath and tried not to whimper.

"Good thing you're so tiny," she said, as she tore the tape off the roll. "Can you imagine trying to tape me up? We'd need to get one of the winches involved." She grinned at me and I laughed, just once. The stabbing started again.

I winced and she made a face. "Sorry."

"It's okay." I moved a little, testing out the situation. "This is better. Thanks."

She shrugged. "I broke a rib once. It starts getting better in a couple of days, but you're going to have a hard time moving around for a while." She held my shirt out to me. "Come on, let's put your titties away."

I laughed again, which still hurt, but I couldn't help it. I realized that I hadn't been embarrassed for even a second. I let her help me get dressed then help me up off the floor. It must have been hilarious to watch, but I was too concerned about jostling myself to think about it much. And I was really going to have to stop laughing at things.

⚓

After a couple of ideas that didn't work, Tulia got me wedged in the corner seat in the main salon. The pain in my ribs had obliterated my upset stomach at least, so I let Jimmy bring me a sandwich and a cup of coffee. I still felt like an idiot. After fussing over me for way too long, I finally convinced Tulia to go back to bed and Jimmy left to finish lunch prep. Once I was left alone, tears stung the back of my nose.

I took a deep breath and forced them back down. I'd done more crying in my short time on the *Byte Bucket* than I had in years and it was a habit I was ready to break. I looked out the porthole while I carefully sipped my coffee and thought.

I didn't think there was much chance of getting down the ladder to the server room in my current state. I thought about getting Martin to check the email at least, but simply explaining how to log in would take most of his down time. It wouldn't be fair to the rest of the crew to make them take on my work as well as their own, especially since there wasn't really anything they could do. If there was a concerted attack on RRD's servers, I couldn't talk any of them through the response. And if there wasn't, it didn't matter.

I sighed. I was just a liability now. A mouth to feed, a body underfoot. Worse than useless.

Mat came through the door. I watched her, wide-eyed, as she walked easily across the space, her body rolling along with the movement of the boat. I tensed, awaiting the chewing-out I so totally deserved. Her face didn't say angry, though, and she sat down next to me softly.

"How you feeling?" Her voice was just loud enough to hear over the sound of the boat creaking and the waves sloshing.

"Stupid," I said without thinking.

She smiled at that and shook her head. "It happens. It's easy to look back and see how it could've been avoided, but that doesn't matter now." She settled back into the cushions and narrowed her eyes as she looked out the port to the horizon. "Good news is that things should settle down soon. The latest weather reports say that the swell should start lying down over the next twelve hours and tomorrow we should even out a lot. That's going to make it a lot easier for you to move around."

"Thanks."

She looked at me, her head cocked to one side. "For what? I didn't order the weather. If only I could!"

I nodded. "Thanks for not yelling at me."

She shrugged. "Like I said, shit happens. Our job is to deal with it when it does." She laid a hand on my shoulder and looked at me intently. "But this is your only freebie. Next time you hurt yourself, you're going overboard."

She kept a straight face for a second then laughed at

my expression. "We've all done it at some time or other. Don't be afraid to ask for help if you need it, okay?" I nodded and she went down below.

If I hurt myself again I'll throw myself overboard, I thought.

⚓

The first day was the worst. I never really made it far from the seat Tulia had stuffed me into and that was just to get to the head. The less said about that process the better. Bending over hurt. Moving my arms hurt. Turning my head too fast hurt. Breathing hurt. I'd never understood just how central to existence a set of ribs actually were.

Every time someone brought me something — a bottle of water, a sandwich, a book — I felt like I had to apologize. After his third visit, Martin finally said, "Look. If you're going to say sorry whenever I come by I'm just going to stop. It's no big deal to bring you stuff but listening to you anyone would think I'd swam back to Ecuador for it. Just chill, already."

"Okay." I gave him a weak smile and he rolled his eyes.

"I'm almost afraid to ask," he said, "but there's got to be something that needs doing with your servers." He dramatically gulped then asked what he could do.

I'd already determined that no one was going to be able to do anything technical, but I could at least be assured that things were working properly. And if they weren't... well, at least I'd know and I wouldn't be sitting here wondering.

"Yeah. There is. It won't be so bad." I walked him through booting up the laptop. Then I explained that there was a log program on the desktop and he just had to open it. I went through the likely things the log would say for the few scenarios I'd projected. "You don't have to memorize this stuff," I said as Martin got more and more perplexed. "Just let me know what it says, okay?"

"I'll try," he said and we went through the shutdown process a couple more times until he nodded.

I read a couple of chapter of my book and was starting to wonder what had happened to him when Martin came back and reported. I smiled and felt the knot of stress in my shoulders unwind just a little. "Everything is working fine," I said. "No change from yesterday."

"You look like you dodged a bullet or something."

"There is something a little weird going on with the system," I explained. "I think it was worrying me more than I realized."

He nodded. "But it's all much ado about nothing?"

"So far," I said and shrugged, then yelped.

Time loses a lot of its meaning when you're on a passage. The rhythm of the watch changes make more sense than the ticks on a clock, and if you're sleeping on a strange schedule you might not even be able to track the transition from day to night. So it was for me while I recuperated. I read books, watched some bad movies, ate sandwiches. Twice I carefully maneuvered myself to my bunk when I got tired but I slept in the main salon a few times, too. The combination of time's healing power and the promised reduction in the waves meant that things just got easier and I eventually decided it was time to try and get down the ladder to the server room.

The boat wasn't moving much at all by now, but I'd learned my lesson — I grabbed those handholds with an iron grip. I carefully maneuvered myself to the ladder, and slowly step-by-stepped my way down, wincing at each time I had to stretch my injured side. It wasn't that bad, though, and I finally got down to the bottom.

After a bit of fiddling I got the workstation unlatched and the laptop secured and booted. Martin had done a fine job of putting everything away and I smiled at how helpful everyone had been. Even Christine had been nice about delivering me soup and sandwiches. If I'd ever deserved one of her needling remarks, it was now. But she was still grateful for the gimballed seat, I guessed, so she kept her opinions of this ignorant landlubber to herself.

It's not like she was wrong, after all — I obviously didn't know what I was doing out here.

The laptop spooled up and I opened the log file. Still loads of traffic, but no change and no faults. Whatever was going on didn't seem to be malicious after all. I let out a breath I didn't realize I'd been holding. I remembered my panicked email to headquarters and fired up the client. It felt like a million years before the new message icon stopped spinning, but eventually there it was — a reply!

I opened it up and finally understood what people meant by a side-splitting laugh. I grabbed my sore ribs and hung on because I couldn't stop laughing.

> Hi, Devi.
>
> Yeah, traffic is up over the all the nodes, but it's nothing to worry about. Just the opposite, actually. We got Boinged! Tripled the customer base overnight and active accounts, too. We've been swamped getting two new nodes up.
>
> FYI, this pushes us up higher on the government's radar, so there might be some interruptions on our end as we make sure that we can stay in operation. No worries, all in a day's work fighting the good fight in the privacy wars!
>
> Hope you're having a good passage and check in when you get to Hiva Oa. We'll send out some upgrades to help you cope. We can afford it!

Anita Running Horse
CTO
Really Remote Desktop

Boing Boing. I should have known it was just a traffic spike due to more users, that explained everything. I guess I'd just forgotten that RRD was a consumer product like anything else — one decent piece of publicity could put our traffic through the roof. And Boing Boing was a blog with a huge readership, many of whom would be ideal customers for RRD.

I didn't like the idea that the US government was going to be monitoring us more closely, though. Even if our work was legal, which as far as I understood it, it was, an investigation could make things very difficult. Still, this was good news. Our problem wasn't an attack. It was success.

⚓

Between my healing ribs, the milder weather and the obvious sense from the rest of the crew that we were nearing our destination, I started to relax. Sleep was coming a lot more easily and I was keeping to a more normal schedule. I tended to join the night watch for a couple of hours after supper, keeping out of the way near the stern of the cockpit and enjoying the night sky until my eyelids began to droop. I started to look forward to that time every day — none of us talked much after sunset. The stars and moon and the dark of the sea had a peaceful serene quality that made us all tend toward quiet introspection.

I was off in my own little world, thinking about space travel and robotic asteroid ore harvesters when something caught my attention. I'd kind of tuned out the sea sound — I guess there's no surprise that waves are commonly used as background white noise. But something had changed and it made me look over the side. At first I couldn't tell what it was, but then I saw it: a flash of green in the water. I must have made a noise of my own because before I knew it Tulia was beside me, hanging her head over the side.

"Oh my god," she said, "look!" I was looking all right. There were several large marine animals, dolphins I guessed, swimming beside the boat. Fluorescent green dripped off them, making their wakes shine in the darkness.

"What is that?"

"Bio-luminescence," Tulia said, awe in her voice. "Stuff in the water that glows, but you can't see it unless the water is disturbed."

"So it's not... whatever those are?"

"Naw, it's the water. Well, microscopic stuff in the water. But look at those guys go!" We watched the lithe creatures twist through the glowing trails and both of us jumped when one surfaced right next to us with a clearly audible *pffft* as it blew out its blowhole. Definitely dolphins.

They made serpentine patterns, swimming in a complex dance with each other that took my breath away. "How come they're hanging out with us?" I whispered, afraid to scare them off.

"They like to play in our wake. We make a different pattern in the water — it's novelty, I guess." We watched them, both of us leaning over the side as much as we dared. We both had our tethers connected to the D rings in the cockpit, so there was no danger of actually falling overboard, but it felt precarious. Finally, after what felt like ages but was still too soon, they moved on, outpacing us effortlessly.

"Wow."

"Yeah," Tulia agreed.

"Have you ever seen that before?"

"Oh sure," she said, "tons of times." She shook her head, a contented smile on her face. "It never gets old."

While she ran through her checklist of things to do on shift I stared out to sea, marvelling at the beauty of the night. A feeling of timelessness came over me, a strange sensation of not replaying about the events of the day or worrying about tomorrow. I was simply there, in the moment, in that place, a tiny part of the vastness of the ocean. I looked up to the stars and felt the same, only magnified beyond human comprehension. We are so small, our little spinning blue dot in the universe, our time so short in the history of the universe.

It should have made me feel insignificant. It should have been depressing. Instead I'd never felt so alive, so utterly *magnificent* in my life.

⚓

After the night with the dolphins, it was like something

switched on in me. I realized that aside from my period of convalescence, I'd been counting every day, paying constant attention to our speed and ETA. When the weather had calmed down everything had gotten a lot more stable, but a part of me had been disappointed that we'd slowed down. After the dolphins, I stopped counting.

Every day I'd get up whenever I happened to wake, enjoy a chat with Jimmy in the galley, then come up to see the world. It was always the same and always different — nothing but sky and sea as far as I could see, but each day the colours would be unique, the shape of the waves a little different. Some mornings the deck would be littered with the bodies of unlucky flying fish that had been waylaid in the night. One day there were tiny squid amongst the casualties. Mat caught a fish. Martin and I took to playing a game of gin rummy in the afternoons before supper. Every day my ribs hurt a little less and I could move easier.

One afternoon I overheard Martin and Tulia talking quietly in the galley as I passed by. "... worried you stayed on board because of me."

"Well, it was an incentive. But, no. Not really. Why? Are you... are we done... ?"

"No, it's just... complicated."

I'd already heard too much and got a move on. I couldn't imagine how hard it must be to start a relationship in such a confined situation. The next day I half expected Martin and Tulia to have some massive fight, or there to be some huge awkward mess between them, but whatever it was they must have resolved it, because everything was normal on board — book reading, telling time by what we were eating, the endless cycle of watch rotation.

It wasn't exactly like being on a beach holiday, but it wasn't normal life either. I couldn't remember the last time the pace of my daily life had been so leisurely. Even on holiday, I'd always been a planner — afraid to miss out on something amazing, I'd fill my days with activity. Now, between three meals, a visit to the server room, afternoon cards and evening stargazing, I felt like my days were as full as they needed to be. It was liberating. I wondered what it would be like when we finally got there.

I wasn't sure I really wanted to get there anymore.

⚓

After two weeks we'd run out of anything resembling a green vegetable. Jimmy had alfalfa seeds, but it was too hot and humid to sprout them — by the time they were big enough to eat they'd already gone mouldy. It sounds like a hardship, but it wasn't really that bad. There were onions and potatoes and canned goods galore. Jimmy had a full spice rack and he knew how to use it. I was amazed every day at the tasty meals he managed to create out of cans and powders.

I had a mouthful of some kind of mild curry made of tomatoes and garbanzo beans when Tulia clattered down the ladder to the gallery. I hadn't seen her for a few days — our schedules had slipped over into the opposite rotation, and I had a warm feeling come over me when I saw her. But when I saw her face it was like I'd been hit by a surprise wave over the gunwale. She looked awful.

I stopped myself from asking the obvious question; when my ribs were hurting I'd found that the last thing I wanted to hear was someone asking how I felt. I guessed she didn't exactly want to know that she looked like shit. I smiled at her, then went back to my curry. She wordlessly made her way to the galley, grunted at Jimmy and came back with her own bowl. She set it on the table then sat down not quite across from me. She stuck her spoon into the bowl, but didn't take a bite, her shoulder slumped over the table.

I couldn't stop myself this time. "You okay?"

She shrugged but didn't look at me. "Yeah. No. I don't know." She leaned back and finally looked up. "I'm not really looking forward to making landfall this time."

I nodded. "I've been thinking the same thing. I'm finally getting the hang of being out here, it's hard to think that it will be over soon."

She frowned. "It's not that. I mean, yeah, it nice out here, but that's not what I mean. I'm just not really ready to go home."

I took a moment to parse what she'd said. "You're leaving the boat?"

She made a face. "I hope not, but my term's just about up."

"Surely they'll renew your contract."

"Probably. But my family will do their best to make

sure I stay on the island and even with a job in hand I don't know if I can fight them."

I must have looked as confused as I felt because Tulia barked a mirthless laugh and said, "We're stopping at Mo'orea. It's where I'm from, my whole family lives there."

"Oh." I felt like an idiot. I'd never even heard of Mo'orea before, which must have been obvious.

"It's an island near Tahiti, part of French Polynesia. My family have a farm there, and my brother manages one of the resorts. Last I heard, his wife was running a tour company. There's a lot of tourism; it's really beautiful and my family has done quite well. They can't understand why I'd ever want to go anywhere else, let alone this." She twirled a finger in the air to indicate the boat.

"Huh." I frowned. "I thought you were like Mat and Isaac — some kind of life long sailor type."

She laughed. "Well, I grew up on the water and I've always been around boats, but it's not like this for islanders. Yachting is kind of a popa'a thing."

"Uh..."

"Didn't you notice in the Galápagos that there weren't too many people who look like you and me?"

"Sure there were," I said, confused.

"On the private boats," she clarified. "Think about the anchorage, the dinghy docks, the bars. See any similarities?"

I hadn't noticed it at the time, but she was right. I guess I was just used to seeing more white people than anyone else in most situations. One of the coolest things about the places we'd been so far was that there were lots of brown people everywhere. But Tulia was right — they were the locals. The other cruisers were almost all white people. We'd met people from Europe, Australia and New Zealand, plus lots of boats from the US and Canada, but they'd almost all been white.

"Whoa."

"The Bucket is unusual in a lot of ways."

I laughed. "Yeah, I'm starting to see that." We both ate in silence for a few moments, then I said, "So, what are you gong to do? About your folks, I mean?"

She shrugged. "I dunno. I thought about asking Mat to skip Mo'orea, but we have to stop at Pape'ete to check in and it's right next door. I can't avoid them, but I don't know what to say." She sighed. "I'll figure something out, I guess."

I felt bad for Tulia, but I knew I was the last person on the boat with anything approaching useful advice. I wondered what it would be like to have a family like that. I would never have even been on this boat if it hadn't been for my family pretty much forcing me to take this job. Intellectually I knew that lots of parents were conservative about wanting their kids to stay at home or learn the family business of whatever, but I didn't *understand* it. Sometimes, I kind of envied the sense of security. But Tulia seemed so miserable that I wonder if it were just one of those things you can't avoid: kids are always pushing against what their parents want, and parents are always disappointed in their kids.

What a depressing thought.

⚓

I'm not going to pretend that a couple of weeks at sea turned me into some kind of mystical sailor or something, but I swear that I could *feel* that we were getting close to land. It wasn't even like approaching the Galápagos, where there was something to see — there was nothing visible out there. But something was different, I knew it.

"Are we getting close?" I finally asked Isaac. I guessed it was mid-afternoon; I'd completely given up clock time.

He nodded. "Tomorrow, actually."

I knew I sounded kind of crazy, but it somehow didn't seem strange to say it out loud. "Yeah, I can feel it, I think."

Isaac nodded again, making no indication that he thought I was nuts. "The ocean shows you," he said cryptically, but I followed the line of his pointed finger. Stuff in the water — seaweed or algae or something, I couldn't tell. His arm raised at the flock of bird which had been pacing us for most of the day. It came to me like finally getting the answer to a tough math problem: there had been nothing to see for so long, a single bird was cause for excitement. Now it was like the ocean was teeming again. It was obvious that something was up.

"Life likes land," Isaac said. "Even the underwater animals flock to the shallows around land. You can always tell when you're coming into a landfall: look for the clouds and the creatures."

I looked in the direction he was staring at and saw an isolated cloud on the horizon off in the distance. "Is that..."

"Yup," he said, a grin spreading across his face. "That cloud is hovering over Hiva Oa."

"... Cool."

I thought about those ancient explorers, setting out on open boats with nothing but the stories told by their seafaring ancestors and a burning curiosity about what was out there. It felt unbelievable that people like the Polynesian settlers ever found anything in the vastness that is the Pacific. But I was learning the signs of the sea, the hints that it was not all the endless ocean that it appeared to be.

It almost made me believe that the world wants us to understand it. Certainly, it's easy to see why people could think that way.

The cloud on the horizon almost seemed to beckon to me.

⚓

I wonder if the fact that places in the world are so *different* ever get old? Hiva Oa was like nowhere I'd ever seen before, even in travel documentaries. Kind of a mountain jutting out of the sea, obviously volcanic, a tall, pointy rock but somehow still lush. It reminded me of stalactites, but upside down and thrusting out of the ocean. It was immense — powerful and raw.

We rounded the island in slow motion. You kind of

lose track of how relatively sluggish six or seven knots is when there's nothing to compare it to, but we slid past the island slowly enough to get the binoculars out and really get a good look at it. This was obviously where our friendly flock of birds called home, as they settled on the tree limbs and bits of rocky outcroppings.

I suspected my jaw was hanging open when I caught Tulia's eyes. She gave me the thumbs up but I could see in her face that she didn't share the rest of the crew's enthusiasm. I smiled in a way that I hoped looked sympathetic, but got distracted by a squeal of delight.

"Shark!"

Sure enough, there was the tell-tale fin slicing through the water about three boat lengths off our side. "Should we be worried?"

"Naw." That was Jimmy. "Not unless you're planning on swimming to Atuona, which I don't recommend since it's still about fifteen miles off."

"Sharks are mostly nocturnal hunters anyway," Mat said, "there's usually not much to worry about."

"Okay. So, Atuona?"

"It's the city..." Tulia barked a laugh and Mat gave her a friendly scowl. "Okay, fine, it's the *town* at Hiva Oa. There's an anchorage there and we have to check in — immigration, customs, that stuff."

"Yeesh, you're going to have another week of line-ups and forms?"

"Not likely. Things are different here. This is France. And these are the islands. Both cultures not known for their officiousness. Last time I was here, when I went to check in, they told me they were closed to go fishing and to come back the next day. It's much more... relaxed than Latin America."

"Than any America," Jimmy said to a set of laughs. "This is the stuff of the movies and books, Devi. Welcome to life in the South Pacific."

It sounded idyllic and I quickly got over my reluctance to make landfall. I was ready for a fresh baguette, ready for some creamy brie. I was ready for a shower and a long walk. I helped the crew tidy up as much as I could as we readied the boat for anchoring. I had an armload of sippy cups and Tupperware that I'd collected form the cockpit and headed down to the galley to help clean and slow them when I bumped right into Tulia coming back up.

Her eyes were red and her cheeks puffy. I opened my mouth to say something, but she shook her head. "I'll figure something out," she said, a catch in her voice.

I nearly freaked out when we turned into the anchorage. I knew that coming to civilization after a couple of weeks of encountering nothing but the *Bucket*, the crew and that one pod of dolphins would make for some adjustment, but I wasn't prepared. At all.

The anchorage seemed tiny, too small for even a few boats. And there were a lot more than a few boats already there. As the bay opened up they were so close I was sure they must be touching. Even I knew that a boat at anchor needs room to swing 360°. There wasn't room for anything in this bay.

I wasn't the only one who was thinking it, I'm sure, and Mat said to no-one in particular, "Mmm. It's a bit crowded. But you anchor bow and stern in here, so we'll find a space. Martin, I need you on the foredeck to ready the primary and Isaac, get the aft anchor ready, please."

I heard a few aye-ayes and there was a flurry of activity. I found a place to park that was out of the way and watched, wide-eyed, as we dropped the sails and started up the engine. We slowed dramatically and then began to pick our way between the other large boats that were in the outer anchorage. There was a breakwater and even more boats in the inner bay. I didn't know how that was possible.

A few revs of the engine and several hand gestures between the bow and the helm later, and we had the main anchor down. Then we let out what felt like all the chain in the world as we backed up halfway out of the bay. Isaac eventually let the aft anchor drop, and then Martin began to pull in the chain he'd just deployed at the bow as we motored forward. Then there was a little fiddling with the bow chain and we were done.

With anchors set bow and stern, we stayed more or less where we were, and didn't swing around with the wind. It felt different than being anchored usually did, but I could see how it meant that a lot more boats could use the same space. "How come people don't always do this?" I asked.

"It's a fairweather anchorage thing," Isaac said. "Also, it's a tricky maneuver." He nodded over to the inner anchorage. "I'd wager that a quarter of those stern anchors are going to drag, more if a breeze kicks up."

"Isn't that kind of dangerous?"

He shrugged. "Yes and no. Bumper boats happens, especially somewhere like this. It's one of the reasons we'll leave someone aboard while we're here."

"Speaking of going ashore..." Mat appeared from down below, freshly showered and changed into the closest approximation of business clothes she seemed to have: a thin, cap sleeved floral shirt that looked like it had been washed a thousand times and brown overalls that looked like a dress from a distance but which were actually loose trousers. She must have seen me staring because she said, "Propriety and sun cover. Everything does two jobs on my boat."

I nodded, pretending to understand.

"I'll get the dinghy prepped," Isaac said, then without waiting for an answer went forward to inflate the dinghy.

"You want to come with me, Devi?" Mat asked.

I looked past the boats at anchor, at the lush trees, the few people walking along the road that skirted the bay and led to what I assumed was town further inland. I could smell chlorophyll and something floral that I couldn't identify.

It was land.

Land, after so long with nothing but sea and sky. Of course I wanted to go with her!

⚓

Inflating the dinghy was a long process, so there was enough time for all of us to shower and change, even though only Mat, Martin, Christine, and I were going ashore. Mat had been running the desalinator whenever it was calm enough, so our water tanks were still full. I understood that some anchorages weren't clean enough to run it, so we tended to make fresh water when we were on the move. As far as I knew, we'd never been low, and one of the perks on landfall day was everyone got a shower, regardless of the usual schedule we followed to keep water usage down.

I found myself still hanging on the the grab bar with one hand while soaping myself with the other even though we were as solid as if we were ashore. I hadn't realized how much I'd acclimatized to the moving boat —

one hand for me, one hand for the ship ingrained in my every move. I actually freaked out a bit when I noticed what I was doing and let go.

There was still a queue for the shower after me, so I went down to the server room to check on the systems. There was a weak cell network available, but the test pings I sent told me that it was better than the satellite so I switched the router. I remembered that I was supposed to check in with Head Office once we'd made landfall, but I didn't feel the urgency any more. I could hardly remember those first few days at sea, when I was so concerned about a possible attack. It seemed laughable now.

I did put my phone on the charge in the hopes of finding some free wifi ashore — I wanted to let my family know that we'd made it. I wonder if they were worried. I'd have been worried if it were one of them, or at least I would have been before. Now... I was starting to understand where Mat and Isaac got their laid-back attitudes.

⚓

Being on solid ground felt weird. It was okay so long as I was walking, but as soon as I stood still it felt like the world was moving. While I waited for Mat to secure the dinghy, I had to put my hand against a nearby tree to stop from falling over.

"You okay?" Martin asked.

"I dunno. I fell kind of wobbly."

"Land sick," Christine said.

"What?"

She shrugged. "I get it, too. Takes a day or so to get used to being ashore. You'll be all right."

"Is it like seasickness?" I asked, concerned. "Am I going to start barfing?"

She shook her head and laughed, but it didn't seem mean. "I doubt it. You just feel weird is all. For me the worst is in a shower, but we're staying on the boat so that won't happen. Come on, let's get walking. That will make you feel better."

We set out along the road and she was right; the sense of vertigo disappeared once I was moving, even if I wasn't moving all that fast. Not having gone for a walk longer than the length of the boat in a couple of weeks had made me a bit slow-moving, but I wasn't alone. None of us were going to win a land-speed record as we walked into town.

It felt like the longest walk of my life, but even though it was hot and I had no idea when, or if, we were ever going to get there, I found that I didn't really mind. Mat kept us entertained by listing off the things she planned to eat.

"First I'm getting a baguette. Soft, fluffy clouds of bread, all hot from the oven. Mmmm. No — ice cream! That's got to be first. Oh, and pamplemousse."

"What?" Martin asked.

"Grapefruit," I said, happy to be able to use the little French I had.

"Yeah, but not like any grapefruit you've ever had,"

Mat said, "sweet and juicy, only a little tart. And it's the size of your head." She held her hands out in a ball gesture, then stopped walking. "I can't believe I forgot! It's got to be a chow mien casse croute!" She took off again with a renewed determination.

"So, which are you having today?" Christine asked when Mat had finally stopped listing food.

Mat gave her a face. "That *is* what I'm eating today!"

"It's a good thing Jimmy isn't here," Christine said, "he'd think you didn't like his cooking."

"Oh, please," Mat said. "I saw that list he gave you for the grocery store. I'm not the only one who's excited about something new."

All this talk of food was starting to make me hungry, so when we turned another corner and instead of trees and mountainside there were building and houses, I found myself speeding up the pace.

"Hold your horses," Mat said, "we have to stop at the Gendarmerie first and we might be a while. We'll get to town soon enough, I promise."

I reined it in, curious about what this would be like. I had a feeling that the official process wouldn't be anything like it was in Costa Rica or the Galápagos.

I was right.

The Gendarmerie was a tidy, white painted building that looked like a regular house whose owners had a minor security fetish. There was a cop car — cop jeep, really — parked outside and a severe-looking fence which I probably could have hopped if I'd wanted to. Mat pushed the buzzer on an intercom and a laconic voice came through. They had a brief and baffling conversation in French, then Mat turned to us.

"I doubt I'll be long, but you can go ahead if you want. Remember that restaurant we passed a couple of blocks back?" Christine nodded. "I'll meet you there in an hour if I don't find you first." Mat didn't wait for an answer as the gate buzzed and she went into the yard of the police station, a riot of colourful flowers rippling in the breeze she made as she walked past them.

"Okay," Christine said, pulling Jimmy's grocery list out of the pocket of her cut-offs. "Let's go shopping."

⚓

Down the road was a bank where we all used the well-worn ATM, walking away with fistfuls of French Polynesian Francs. "So, where to?"

"There's a grocery store up the way," Christine said.

"You've been here before?" Martin asked.

She shook her head and pulled out what looked like a page torn out of a Lonely Planet guidebook. We started walking, then Martin said, "So, anyone speak French?"

Two sets of eyes turned to me and my face got hot. "Uh..." French might be one of Canada's official languages, but outside a government office, you'd never know it where I lived. I'd taken French in junior high, but I wasn't exactly good with languages. I'd tried Mandarin in high school, but that was even worse. "I can say bonjour."

"That'll have to do," Martin said with a grin. What

had I gotten myself into?

Until I saw the first few other people walking around I hadn't noticed how eerily empty the street had been until now. But once we turned the corner, there were about a half dozen people milling around, and I had to stop myself from being the asshole tourist standing there gawping at the locals.

I'm from Vancouver. There is no shortage of tattooed people in that city, and I thought I was accustomed to seeing ink on skin. It never really occurred to me that there would be places where almost every person would be tattooed — the little old lady sitting outside the bakery with her grandchildren, ancient complex tattoos covering both arms. The middle-aged guy wearing nothing but surf shorts, with no part of his body that I could see unadorned, including his face. The pretty girls almost my age, their hair, clothes and makeup out of any North American teen magazine, but with traditional-looking tattoos on their shoulders. Large looping swirls, delicately inlaid with geometric designs that reminded me of scrimshaw.

"Jeez," I said, under my breath. "The people here are beautiful."

Christine heard me and laughed. "You can see why all those dirty old French artists came here and didn't want to ever leave."

I nodded, but felt an uncomfortable flush come over me. I was doing the very thing that I hated when it happened to me. And it happened to me a lot. *You have such beautiful skin, bi-racial people get the best genes, don't you think?* Ugh. I hated being treated like an exotic food and I really didn't want to do that to someone else.

"It's hard to remember that everyone is just people, you know," I said, "especially when everything is so different."

Martin nodded. "That's the point of travel, though, right? To learn about the differences and explore the similarities?"

"I guess."

"Well, I want to explore some food," Christine said. "Same, different, I don't even really care that much anymore. I'm starving!"

We walked into the bakery, which we must have been smelling for a block before we found it. There were regular loaves of sandwich bread up on shelves behind the counter, some small pastries, but the place was dominated with buckets full of classic French baguettes. I looked over to Martin and Christine, who shrugged at me. I screwed up my courage — I'd always hated trying to speak another language. But I wanted a baguette!

"*Une baguette, s'il vous plait?*" The lady behind the counter smiled at my doubtless mangling of what would probably be the easiest sentence I could have started with. She told me the price slowly, and I still didn't get it exactly, but handed her a couple of hundred franc notes. She grinned fully now, handing me back one of the bills I'd given her along with some coins from the register.

"*Merci,*" I said.

"Thank you," she answered in better English than my French and we all blushed. "'Ave a good day."

We left the bakery and I said, "Next time I'm not going anywhere without Mat. How do you guys manage it in all these strange places where you don't speak the language?"

"What do you mean 'all these places'?" Martin said. "It's been all Spanish so far and I get by. I mean, I've got menu Spanish down pat, and mostly that's all I've needed."

Christine rolled her eyes. "And I've been around to bail you out." She chucked him on the shoulder. "But I've been a few places where I've got nothing — Turkey, Italy. You can get pretty far with *hello*, *goodbye*, *yes*, *no*, *where is the bathroom* and hand gestures."

"*Où est la salle de bain*," I said. "Repeat after me."

We sat under a tree and ate the fresh bread by the handful. It was warm and fluffy and somehow tasted simultaneously exotic and homey. Maybe we were just hungry, because the entire metre-long stick disappeared in no time.

"Okay, that was easily the best bread I've ever eaten," Martin said. "How much did it cost?"

I looked through the change I'd gotten. "Uh, 70 francs." I made a face.

"Whoa," Christine said.

"Yeah," I said, "but it was worth it."

She looked at me funny. "Um, Devi, one franc is like one cent. That wasn't even a dollar."

"I guess I should have taken out more than five hundred francs then."

"Speaking of which, do we have time to hit the grocery store before we meet Mat?"

I pull out my phone and waited while it found a tower and updated with the time. "Is half an hour enough?"

"Sure," Christine said, standing up. "If we get a move on."

We walked back past the bakery and into a tiny shop. It was about the size of an average hotel room, crowded with bare wooden shelves that had hardly enough space for a single person to walk between them. They were filled with unfamiliar packaged goods. Luckily, while having a conversation in French was an embarrassment, living in Canada I'd learned food names by osmosis. I looked around the store, then grabbed a large flat tin.

"You guys!" I held it up for Martin and Christine to see. "This is *duck*. In a *can!*"

"Is that on Jimmy's list?" Martin deadpanned and Christine actually looked at the paper.

She shook her head. "We should mention it when we get back," she said. "Who knows with that guy, he might have a great duck a l'orange recipe in his back pocket."

I could have easily hung out in the store a lot longer, enjoying all the foreign packages and odd foods. It was definitely French and almost all obviously imported.

There wasn't much in the way of fresh stuff — I wondered where people got fruit and vegetables from. Maybe they just fell off the trees?

Christine took her few items up to the counter and paid, packing everything up in a knapsack to take back to the boat. "Let's get another couple of baguettes on our way back," she said. "Something to go with all this cheese!"

⚓

Mat was already at a table when we got to the *snack* — the local term for a little café/diner. She had a Hinano in front of her and a plate of french fries, both nearly gone. "Manna from heaven," she said pointing at what was left on the table as we sat down. "You guys hungry?"

"We ate a loaf of bread," Martin said, sounding a bit like he'd been caught with his hand in the cookie jar, but Mat just nodded as if that were the most normal thing in the world.

"You left a couple of sticks for later," she said, glancing at the knapsack. "Surprising restraint." She grinned and slugged down the last of her beer. "You okay to head back to the Bucket?" We all nodded and she scarfed down the last of the fries. "Good. I don't know how much longer I'm going to make it before I have to sleep for a half a day."

She paid the shy teenager at the register and we trooped the long road back to the dinghy. We shared the burden of the knapsack on the walk, but it was still long and hot. I hadn't thought I was particularly tired, but

Mat's comment about wanting to sleep had brought out a level of fatigue that was increasing was every footstep. It was a beautiful walk, though I was grateful when I saw the wooden Bienvenue á Hiva Oa sign that was near where everyone stowed the dinghies.

The tide had gone out since we'd arrived and the concrete ramp where we'd dragged the dinghy up had a few centimetres of slime near the bottom. "Ugh," Mat said. "That's going to be fun." We maneuvered the dinghy down into the water and carefully one-by-one'd it into the boat. Martin slipped and so did I, but miraculously neither of us ended up in the drink. Once we were putt-putting back to the Byte Bucket I noticed that I'd scraped my leg a little, but it didn't hurt.

"You clean that as soon as we get aboard," Mat said when she saw the scrape. "Broken ribs are one thing, an infection is another."

"I will," I said, too tired to find the thought of getting an infection in my leg from gross sea slime even a little bit worrisome.

Jimmy provided me with gunk for my leg scrape, but much more importantly, he provided us all with a feast. While we'd been ashore he'd pulled some fish from the freezer and hauled the barbecue out of its storage locker and set it up. The smell traveled over the bay as we returned and my stomach growled. Apparently that baguette hadn't really done the job after all.

The supplies he'd asked Christine to get augmented the meal: fresh bread, strong cheese, pâté, a tomato and onion salad. It wasn't that different from what we'd been eating on passage, but the novelty of being all together and the few new ingredients made it seem like a party. And it was, I guess.

Mat passed around cans of beer to whoever wanted them, and cracked open the rum for me and Jimmy. Isaac and Mat compared the passage to other ones; apparently we'd made good time. Christine savoured her beer and cheese, Martin revelled in how stable the boat was. I wasn't sure what I thought. It hadn't really hit me yet, I guess. I was happy to be comfortable, happy to be full of food and in good company. I was looking forward to a good night's sleep. I started to wonder if I was even going to make it until it got dark.

Tulia did her best to join in the subdued but still celebratory mood. "Oh my god, pâté!" She took a fork to it and ate a mouthful without even spreading it on any bread, her eyes closing and a smile appearing on her face. "I don't even know how long it's been," she said dreamily once she'd swallowed. Then a shadow crossed her face and I caught her eye. She shrugged almost imperceptibly, then seemed to push her feelings down, taking a plate and loading it up with bread, cheese, and the lion's share of the pâté. She took a spot next to me, a little bit away form the others. Quietly, she said, "I guess if I'm going to have to deal with the bad part of being back home, I might as well enjoy the stuff I've missed, right?"

"Yeah."

The sun dropped down below the horizon as the local time hit about seven pm. There were three other boats anchored in the outer area where we were, and they all had crew enjoying their evenings above decks. The night was early, we all knew it, but celebrating our successful landfall couldn't banish the bone-tiredness I felt. I was just about to admit defeat when Isaac stood.

"I don't know about you, but I can't stay awake another five minutes. I'm going down — see you all in the morning."

"I'm right behind you," Mat said and everyone else nodded their agreement. We cleared up dinner in record time and I don't even remember getting snugged into my bunk before falling into a dreamless, solid sleep.

⚓

The dinghy was low in the water as most of us headed into shore. Jimmy and Christine stayed behind. Jimmy said he wanted to get some stores repositioned and offered to stay. Christine lost the epic rock/paper/scissors tournament we'd all undertaken to determine who got boat duty. Well, everyone but me. If anything actually happened I'd be more of a liability aboard.

I actually felt kind of bad when Mat said I wasn't going to share in the anchor watch. I'd started to feel like I was really part of the crew and being singled out like that smarted more than I'd expected. I made a joke about making sure I never learned enough to be useful, then took myself down to the server room. A few minutes earning my keep might help me feel like less of a burden. Plus, I didn't think my fake smile was going to last much longer.

There was no hint of wifi out in the anchorage, and I'd only noticed a couple of access points ashore. There were cell towers, though, so I made sure the system was connected and checked the logs and messages. Traffic was down a tiny bit — probably just the natural slowdown after a bunch of new customers.

No new email, but the last message from HQ was still in the inbox, reminding me not only that I probably ought to check in with them at some point, but also how much my panic over the unusual traffic flow freaked me out. It seemed ridiculous now. I reminded myself that at the time I hadn't had the full picture, that I was still learning the job, still learning how to be on the boat. Hell, I still didn't even know enough to be trusted to hang around and... yeah. I didn't really even know why they were leaving someone aboard. So, that explained that, I guess.

I stowed the laptop and workstation and tried to remember what it was like getting Martin's help when I couldn't get down here. There's no shame in not knowing how to do something. I knew that perfectly well, but couldn't help but feel like my ignorance of the boat was more like a personality flaw than a simple lack of knowledge.

I looked around the small space that represented pretty much everything I was competent at on board. I was going to be living here for several more months. I couldn't see myself being contented with being the boss of the server room and completely reliant on others everywhere else. I didn't think I was going to become some kind of master sailor, but it was time I learned to do a few things above decks.

Of course, then I nearly dumped everyone out of the dinghy when I slipped getting in. Yeah, I was going to be lucky to ever become more than a liability.

We got ashore without further incident, and only a few cracks about me not making any sudden moves. Martin jumped out as we approached the ramp at the concrete wharf and we all piled out — carefully — then dragged the dinghy up to the top and nestled it next to others just like it under the trees. It was a few hours before the heat of noon would be on us, but it was already hot. I wished I had something with more coverage than my baseball cap, but it was better than nothing.

"Everyone ready for the long march?" Isaac asked,

to nods.

"Hang on." Tulia had her hand on Martin's shoulder as she took off one of her hiking sandals and shook a rock free. "Okay," she said, getting it back on. "I'm ready now."

We'd just started walking when a truck came barrelling down the road from town. "That's odd," Mat said. "I thought there wasn't Le Truck here anymore."

"Le Truck?"

"It's like a taxi," Isaac explained. "But I don't think that's Le Truck." There wasn't anything this far down the dead-end road except the wharf and there was no sign of a large ship. There was no reason for a local to be driving down here. We all looked at each other, confused, then I saw Tulia's eyes get wide.

"No—"

The truck stopped in the middle of the road, and three people rushed out speaking a barrage of French mixed with an assonant language I didn't recognize. They were an older couple dressed much like the shopkeepers we'd seen in town along with a younger man in spotless, neatly pressed linen shorts and a bright floral shirt. They all surrounded Tulia, alternately hugging and seemingly berating her.

"What's going on?" Isaac asked, as Martin stood to the side, confusion all over this face.

"I think we're going to have to change our plans," I said. "Looks like we're going to a family reunion."

After a multilingual introduction that I don't think anyone understood, Tulia's parents and brother apparently agreed to drive us all into Atuona in return for giving them some time with her. She didn't look thrilled, but what could she do? What could any of us do? We climbed into the bed of the truck and rode into town.

They dropped us off at the small museum and her brother, who spoke perfect English, told us that he would be happy to drive us back to the wharf when we were ready to go. "We will be at the snack with Tu. Come by whenever you're ready."

I gathered that "whenever we were ready" should be some time from now and I tried to catch Tulia's eye to offer some kind silent support, but her parents had her in some deep conversation. Martin stepped forward, as if to join them, but I pulled him back. Mat thanked Rainui, Tulia's brother, and they took off in the truck.

"I don't envy her," Mat said.

"Why? What's going on?" Martin looked both pissed at me and bewildered about the entire situation. I was amazed that Tulia hadn't said anything to him about it, but I wasn't about to tell her story behind her back.

Mat clearly had the same thought, since she just made a noise and said, "It's her business, not ours. Come on, let's go for a walk. There's some cool statues around here if I remember right."

⚓

We walked through the cemetery which was strangely attractive with its palm trees, flowers and clay and stone graves. I don't know much about art, but even I recognized Paul Gaugin's name when we came across his grave and its hand-lettered marker. "There's a museum here devoted to him," Mat said. "It's interesting if you like his art, but there aren't originals or anything. If you want to go, you should probably do it today. I'm planning on moving on tomorrow or the next day."

"So soon?" I was surprised. We'd only just gotten here.

Mat shrugged. "There's isn't much here and the anchorage is pretty terrible. I want to stop at a nice beach spot I know for a night or two then go to Nuku Hiva. There's better provisioning and a sail loft at Taiohae and we need some gear."

"Oh." I wasn't ready to move on already, but I didn't have any say in the matter.

"Anyone want to do the museum?" Isaac asked. "I'm going."

I shrugged. "It's not really my bag." Isaac didn't look too upset that I wasn't keen and turned to Martin who made a face.

"Yeah, me either. Sorry."

"No worries," Isaac said. "I'll see you all back at the snack in a couple of hours." He gave us all a wave then headed off down the sandy lane.

Martin looked at me, still clearly pissed, then turned to Mat. "What are you up to, captain?"

"Casse-croute."

I didn't know what that meant, and I don't think Martin did either, but we followed her back toward town anyway. We stopped at the small square, where there was a cart selling sandwiches. Although, "sandwich" isn't really the most descriptive word for an entire baguette filled with the strangest fixings. My stomach was growling, but I didn't think there was any chance I could eat a whole one.

"Want to share one?" I asked Mat, who gave me a look like I'd asked her to split her paycheque or something.

"I am not sharing." She turned her back on us and began chatting with the proprietor in rapid-fire French.

"I'll guess I'll share," Martin said to me, "so long as it's the sausage and french fries one."

We waited for Mat to get her sandwich, which looked enormous and a little bit terrifying, then I muddled through ordering "*une casse-croûte avec saucisse et frites.*"

"What *is* that?" Martin asked when Mat came up for air.

"Chow mien," she said, then took another huge bite.

"Chow mien? Like noodles and stuff? In a sandwich?" She just nodded and kept chewing, a look of concentration and bliss coming over her face.

"*Ma'm'selle?*" I turned and caught sight of mine and Martin's order.

"*Merci,*" I said, my eyes probably goggling out of my head. There were three whole sausages nestled in the split of the baguette, then a massive amount of golden french fries crammed in the rest of the available space.

"That is..." Martin seemed at a loss for words.

"Amazing." I took a bite. It was as good as you'd imagine. Maybe better. I understood why Mat hadn't wanted to share, though I couldn't see myself finishing even half of this one. I passed it over to Martin who accepted the sandwich as a peace offering, and ate with a far off look in his eye. He mumbled something with his mouth full that I couldn't make out but totally understood. I bet the three of us looked like we hadn't seen food in a month, the way we stood there and worked at our sandwiches.

Somehow Martin and I polished off ours and soon enough Mat was wiping her mouth and making small satisfied noises. "How did you eat all that?" I asked.

She narrowed her eyes. "I may be small, but I'm a good eater."

"I see that!"

She laughed. "I probably won't need supper, though."

"For a few days."

We walked around town for an hour, partly to work off the casse-croutes and partly to make sure that Tulia and her family had enough time to do whatever they needed to. "You think she's okay?" I asked Mat at one point when Martin had gone off to look at a stone carving.

Mat shrugged. "She tell you about them?"

"A little."

She nodded. "Well, I don't know that much about her situation, but I know that if we were in Haiti right now and my family turned up at the wharf, I'd probably have turned the dinghy around, gunned the motor, and weighed anchor." I raised my eyebrows. "Supportive parents aren't really that common."

"I guess not."

Mat waved Martin over. "Let's head back — Isaac's probably on his way now and..." She didn't finish the thought, but I guessed that she didn't think it would be fair to let him deal with the Tulia situation on his own.

When we arrived at the small restaurant, there was no sign of Isaac. Tulia and her family, though, had taken over a large table in the corner. By the mostly empty plates, glasses and napkins strewn over the table, they'd been busy and hadn't left. There was a lot of talking going on and a little wild gesticulating, so we hung back a bit until Tulia noticed us standing near the door.

I wasn't sure exactly what the look on her face meant — resignation, relief, just plain tiredness — but she appeared pleased to see us and stood, waving us over. I caught Mat's eye and she made a face as we trooped over to the table. Tulia switched into all French, for Mat's benefit I assumed, and held a brief conversation with Mat and what I guessed were her parents. Martin and I stood nearby, occasionally looking at each other with bewilderment, until Isaac barged through the door.

"Hi, everyone," he said loudly, interrupting whatever negotiations were being carried out by the Francophones. "We probably ought to be getting back, don't you think, Mat."

I wonder if she was going to give him shit for interrupting, but smiled and said, "Definitely." Switching back to French she said something to the older couple and Tulia shrugged and stood. There was a brief flurry of language and arms and hugging, then somehow were were all in the truck hurtling along the high coastal road back to the wharf.

⚓

Conspicuously no one said anything about Tulia's family. Even Martin, who was still cranky and clueless, caught enough of the vibes to know to keep his mouth shut. Jimmy had laid out a great lunch spread, but there was no chance I was eating any of it. He didn't seem upset about it, though. "I remember my first casse-croute," he said, a wistful look in his eye. "I'll say this for the French — they know how to eat."

"Well, I'm not French and I know how to eat, too." Christine elbowed her way to the table and began loading up a plateful. "Some of us didn't get a shore meal." She smiled as she said it though, and I fought not to take it personally .

"Anyone up for a dip?" Isaac walked into the main salon with the snorkel gear in one hand and a bag full of what looked like kitchen tools in the other.

"Sure," I said, "I could stand to cool off a bit."

He frowned at me. "I was thinking of a working swim." He hefted the hardware. "We need to scrape the bottom."

I couldn't quite parse what he meant, then Martin

elbowed me, knocking the dumb look off my face. "We're going to scrape the slime and stuff off the bottom of the boat."

"Oh." I'd noticed a layer of green goo along the edge of the boat at the waterline when I'd gotten in the dinghy, but it hadn't occurred to me that we would do something about it. I looked at Isaac's bag of tools, and figured that I could probably help. If I was going become useful, I might as well start now. "I'll give it a try."

"You don't have to," Isaac said.

"I know. But I do want a swim and I might as well help out if I'm going to be down there anyway."

"Okay. Go get changed and I'll see you on deck."

I go changed quickly and met Isaac on the swim step. Along with the usual snorkel gear, I was issued a heavy spatula on a string, a pair of plastic kitchen gloves and earplugs.

"You don't want to get that stuff stuck in your ears." I didn't really want to think about how Isaac learned that trick, and crammed the plugs in. I got suited up in the rest of the gear and couldn't help but laugh at what I must look like. Martin came up and I asked him to go get my phone for a photo. I'd been terrible about sending pictures back to my family and this was too good to pass up.

After my photo shoot, I jumped overboard along with Isaac, Martin, and Tulia. Isaac showed me how to scrape off the green slime, telling me not to worry about barnacles or the other stubborn shellfish. He brandished a putty knife and said that he'd be taking care of the detail work.

"Just make a quick pass over the slime," he said. "Once it's gone, it's harder for other stuff to grow. Be careful around anything that pokes out of the hull — I've taken out a few depth sounders in my day, and we don't want that. Err on the side of caution, okay?"

I nodded and started swimming along the hull. The spatula took off the goo pretty well and it was nice to do something that had such a tangible and obvious outcome. So much of IT work is slow, full of trial and error, and without a finite end. Watching the lines of clean boat appear where I'd swum was surprisingly satisfying. Scraping gunk off the bottom of the boat felt almost like a treat.

In my maiden snorkelling trips back in Costa Rica I'd leaned to dive underwater and used the technique to continue on to the lower part of the boat. The water was pretty murky with all the crap we were scraping off, so I couldn't really see what it looked like until I swam away for a moment to adjust my snorkel and mask. When I dove back down I was taken aback — I knew the boat had a big heavy keel that kept it balanced, but I'd never thought about what it would look like.

The boat's underside was smooth and round, almost like a whale's belly, tapering to a point at the bow but large at the stern where the scary-looking propellor was located. Isaac was hanging on to part of the keel with one hand scraping away carefully at the prop with the other, while Martin and Tulia swam around with their tools. They reminded me of those fish that some salons use for eating the dead skin off rich people's feet. I laughed out loud, which just meant that I got a mouthful of seawater through my snorkel and had to surface to cough.

When we all got back on board I was amazed to discover that we'd been done there over an hour. "That's a lot of hull," Tulia said as she handed me the half-empty solar shower bag. I opened the tap and let a dribble of hot water pour over me, washing off the salt.

"Yeah," I said. "That was more work that I expected." I stretched under another quick rinse. "I'm kind of sore."

"Thanks for helping out," she said and I nodded. It felt good to help; it even felt good to be sore.

We sat on the foredeck, drying ourselves in the heat of the sun. "So..."

She sighed. "It's not great. I thought I'd have a week or more before I had to deal with them but they've been waiting for us. Rainui offered me a job with his tourism business. When I left he was working at a resort and his wife had a business driving people around the island, but now they both work in the business. They have a staff, several jeeps, even a charter plane — that's how they were able to get to Hiva Oa."

"Wow. They sound really successful."

She nodded. "My brother was always ambitious, but he didn't believe in leaving home to become successful. That's what most of the keeners do — go to France, go to

Australia. But not my brother. And that's part of the problem."

I frowned. "Is that what they think you did?"

She looked out over the bay, away from shore, toward the open water. "It's kind of what I did do."

We both sat there for a minute or an hour, staring at the distance.

"So, what's going to happen now?"

She looked at me, and I wondered if she was going to cry. We were both saved from that moment by Isaac.

"Dinner is what's going to happen now. Then everyone gets a good night's sleep. I just talked to Mat. We're weighing anchor in the morning."

I'd been worried that it was going to be another dawn departure, but I was up before Mat for the only time ever at anchor. I meandered into the galley to find Jimmy and Christine with a pot of coffee and a box of long-life milk on the galley table. I poured a cup and drank half of it without any of us saying a word.

"So—" Christine broke the silence.

"I don't think we're going far," Jimmy said. "Mat gets weird after a long passage. We're all working so hard to get there and then we're there and then what? Once the cold beer and burger hole gets filled, I think she gets freaked out by civilization. We often head for a little gunk hole for a day or two before we make for the busier ports."

"Are you divulging all my secrets?" Mat appeared in the doorway, creases from her pillow still visible on her face. She poured some coffee then scowled at Jimmy. "Breakfast?"

"Aye aye, cap'n!" He winked at me, then started pulling things out of lockers. Soon the table was covered with day-old baguettes he must have hidden, jam, canned butter and some of the cheese. "Thought I might scramble a few eggs, too."

"Eggs." Mat nodded once and sat down to tear into the baguette. Jimmy looked at me and Christine expectantly and I nodded.

"None for me," Christine said. "I'm good here."

"Okay." He busied himself in the kitchen and by the time the rest of the crew rolled in a pan of creamy eggs was steaming on the table. We ate companionably — even Tulia looked more contented than I'd seen her in days.

Once we were all fed, I helped Jimmy stow the galley while the others readied the boat for departure. I hardly noticed as they raised the anchors and we motored out of the bay.

⚓

Leaving was strange. On one hand, being underway had become what I thought of as our default state. It had been a relaxing change to have a couple of nights at anchor, but the sound of waves slapping the sides, the creak of the lines and snap of wind in the sails along with the now-familiar roll of the boat in the swells just felt right. On the other hand, sailing into the bay at Atuona had been the goal we'd been working so hard toward on our passage. It seemed odd to be leaving so soon.

I turned to watch the bay recede into the distance behind us. If Jimmy was right about Mat being freaked out by land, I felt like I maybe understood. I wondered if sailing was the ultimate expression of the grass always being greener — underway, you're focussed on the destination, but in port one eye is always on the horizon. It struck me that I might be hitting on some kind of universal truth of the human condition, but before I could get too philosophical Isaac told me unceremoniously to get the hell out of the way of the jib sheet winch, so I went down to the server room.

We still had a connection to the cell towers on Hiva Oa, so I finally replied to headquarters. I tried to keep it brief, but we didn't have the bandwidth to send them the logs, so I had to try and make a narrative. Writing wasn't exactly my strong suit, but in a couple of dense paragraphs I thought I'd gotten across the jump in traffic, how the servers had managed it, and my best projection for future capacity. I got the impression that our upcoming passages would be shorter, but that our port calls would be more remote, so I guessed that we'd be relying on the satellite provider most of the time. Sticking to a conservative estimate seemed like the right thing to do.

It didn't make for very good reading.

I couldn't see how I was going to manage with even a slight increase in traffic. It was fine for now — we'd seen a small decrease since the initial spike that had worried me after we'd left the Galápagos — but if we got any more press or one of our existing customers decided to get serious, we would be boned.

There wasn't anything I could do about it, of course, so I sent my report off, checked that everything at my end was as shipshape as I could make it, and stowed the gear. The whole process had taken about forty-five minutes, and when I came up above decks I'd completely lost my bearings. It took me a minute with the electronic chart to find Hiva Oa among the islands behind us. I wasn't used to so much land and I found it strangely unnerving.

⚓

There were several other boats in Hanamoenoa Bay and we were by far the largest. We anchored way out from shore, making sure not to crowd any of the boats already parked. Unlike our previous anchorage, there was plenty of room to swing and I needed the binoculars to check out the shore. I couldn't make out any sign of permanent human habitation — I saw a few people that looked very much like they'd come off the boats at anchor walking along the shallow beach, but that was it. It reminded me a little bit of the small beach at Santa Elena in Costa Rica, the first place we'd gone after I joined the crew of the Bucket. That felt like a million miles away, a million years ago.

It didn't take long to get the boat squared away and the dinghy in the water.

"Anyone up for a trip to the beach?"

Mat stayed behind while the rest of us piled in the dinghy. We fit, but only barely, and Isaac drove slowly to the beach. It was like something out of a postcard — turquoise water leading up to creamy golden sand, ringed by lush palm trees. The only thing that marred the almost artificial scene were the dinghies pulled up on the beach. We added ours to the row and set about exploring.

Martin and Tulia took off toward a small path that led into the trees and I felt a pang as I watched them go. I knew that now, especially, they wanted some time to themselves, but I was curious about what Tulia was going to do. And, if I was being honest with myself, I missed

Martin a little bit too. When we were on passage there had been so much free time and I'd grown accustomed to our afternoon gin rummy games. It was nice just hanging out, even if we didn't talk about anything of consequence. I stood there watching the space where they'd been standing and didn't notice Christine coming up behind me.

"I can't convince you to join me in a few asanas, can I?"

It was an overture of peace, but I hated yoga. "Sorry," I said, "not my thing. If we ever find the space and a day when it isn't like breathing jello, want to go for a run sometime?"

She looked at me and raised an eyebrow. "Why not? I used to run on the treadmill, but it's been a while."

"Me, too," I said. "Besides, who knows if we'll ever find a decent day for it."

"Yeah," she agreed, then went off in search of a flat piece of beach. I turned to give her space and began walking along the shore in the other direction. Jimmy and Isaac were ahead of me, closely investigating some of the trees. Everyone had a purpose for being there but me. I had gotten used to that feeling, but I didn't like it.

I walked over to them and said, "Whatcha looking at?"

"Free food!" Jimmy held his hands out to me and opened them. His palms were cupped and full of tiny yellow-green spheres.

"Limes," Isaac explained.

"Cool. So, can we just take them?"

"Sure," Isaac said. "This is public land and there are more here than anyone can use. He pointed at the ground around the trees and I saw heaps of limes that had fallen off the tree in various states of decay. "Waste not want not. You have pockets in those shorts?"

I nodded and began to pick a few limes from the trees. I got about a half dozen in each pocket. "Anything else growing here?"

"I don't think so," Jimmy said. "Maybe some coconuts, but they are harder to get, and these will do for now. No scurvy for us!"

Isaac laughed and we walked back to the dinghy to deposit our prize in one of the battered coolers that Jimmy had brought along. A middle-aged couple were wrestling with their dinghy nearby. They stopped as we approached.

"Which boat are you from?" the tall woman asked.

"Byte Bucket," I answered.

"The big one," Jimmy added, gesturing out toward where we were anchored.

Her eyes widened. "The one with the... interesting paint job?"

I nodded. The *Bucket* had a garish shark face painted on the bow, making it look like we were taking a bite out of the ocean.

"Yeah. Byte Bucket." I overemphasized the first word of the boat's name.

"Okay, then." She chuckled.

The man with her asked, "How many crew do you have?"

"There's seven of us," Isaac said.

The two looked at each other, some kind of silent conversation taking place in the glance. "We can do seven," the guy said finally. "Want to come over for sundowners? We're on *Wildflower*." He pointed at a well-kept ketch not far from shore.

"I don't think the captain has plans," Isaac said and nodded. "I think we'll be there. I'll stop by earlier if things change."

"I'll bring some nibbles and drinks," Jimmy said. "See you then."

"Great." They resumed hauling their dinghy down and were soon rowing back to their boat.

"Sundowners?" I asked.

"Drinks, snacks, hanging out. You know, like we did at Huevos, with *S Cargo*."

"Oh." I'd almost forgotten about out last boat party, but that had been with people that Isaac and Mat had known previously. It seemed pretty clear that these two had never met any of the Bucket's crew before.

Martin and Tulia arrived then, looking both flushed and slightly morose. I didn't get the sense that they'd been arguing, but they weren't exactly radiating happy young love. I wasn't about to ask, though. Christine must have seen us all hanging around the dinghy because she came over, too.

"We've got an invitation for a boat party tonight on

Wildflower," Isaac told them. "We'll have to check with Mat, but it's probably on. Let's get back now and make sure there isn't anything we need to do."

⚓

Mat had no problem with going for a visit and even acted like she welcomed the invitation. I was having trouble getting a handle on her. Earlier in the day I'd decided that she must just be an introvert who needed some down time, but now the prospect of visiting new people seemed to perk her up.

Jimmy was in his element in the galley, doing something with a bunch of the limes we'd gathered, and Christine disappeared into the engine room. Isaac and Martin puttered around above decks, tidying and inspecting the rigging. I checked the server room quickly, but there were no messages and the connection to the satellite network was fine, so that left me at a loose end. I was heading back to my bunk to get a book when I ran into Tulia.

"Hey."

"Hey."

"You okay?"

She shrugged. "My family isn't going to be happy that I just left like that. I told them that it would probably go that way, but... you know."

"Yeah."

"And Martin—" She looked down the corridor as if to see if he were around the corner. "He wants to talk to them, try and get them to understand. As if that's not going to make things worse. My kind-of boyfriend that I'm technically living with telling my parents that I should stay here with him. Please." She laughed once and shook her head. "I know he wants to do something to help, but really. That kind of help I don't need."

"We all want to help," I said. "Maybe Mat..."

"No. It's my decision and it's my problem. Mat can't make me stay, can't pretend that I don't have the ability to leave the boat if I want to. And I can't ask her to get in the middle of this."

I didn't have anything to say to that, didn't have any useful advice or any brilliant ideas. So I just reached out and squeezed her shoulder once.

"Thanks for letting me unload on you."

"Anytime," I said. "After the ribs thing, I kind of owe you one." She laughed, this time for real.

⚓

It took two trips in the dinghy to get us all over to *Wildflower*. Between the cases of beer Mat loaded in and the bags of food Jimmy hauled up from the galley, there was no way we could do it in one shot. So I let the advance party go ahead and waited around on the *Bucket* with Martin and Tulia.

We were conspicuously not talking about her family, so I came up with another topic for discussion. "Am I the only one who thinks it's a bit weird for a couple of total strangers to invite us all over for drinks? I mean, they ran into us totally by chance. What's up with that?"

Tulia looked at me like I was the weirdo, but Martin

said, "It's different on the water. It's like we're part of this floating small town that keeps splitting up and reforming in new configurations, but we're all one community. So just because we haven't met *Wildflower* before, they're still essentially neighbours. Does that make any sense?"

"I guess." I wasn't sure, though.

"It isn't just boat people, though," Tulia said, giving Martin a bit of side eye. "Islanders aren't wary of new people so much. Maybe it's because it's such a journey to get anywhere around here, but we all tend to be curious and welcoming of new people. Strangers are an excuse to have a feast, to have a party. Seems to me that's all Wildflower is doing — using us as an excuse to have a social time. After all, what's the point of traveling if you don't meet new people?"

She had a point. Though, I had to admit, until then I'd never given much thought to the point of travel. I wasn't exactly here because of itchy feet. Isaac was on his way back with the dinghy, so we got ready to load into the boat. We sped over to *Wildflower* where food was already arranged in their small cockpit and drinks were in flow.

I clambered up the ladder and made my way to the cockpit. The Bucket's crew filled it with only a couple of seats left. The tall woman who'd invited us caught my eye and grinned. "Hi," she said, sticking a hand out for me to shake. "I'm Lise."

"Devi," I said, preparing for explanation, but she just nodded.

"That'll be easy to remember," she said, turning

toward the guy passing out drinks. "He's Dave."

He looked up at the sound of his name, slightly confused. "Hi, I'm Devi," I said, raising my hand in a wave. He was taken aback for a second then laughed.

"Of course," he said. "Seems like every other person I meet out here is Dave or David. There had to be one among you, right?" I laughed and nodded. "What can I get you?"

I looked over the drinks table and asked for a rum and juice. In short order he passed me over a nice shatterproof glass and I found a slice of seat to wedge into.

The rest of the introductions were made, then we settled into what I realized was the usual getting to know you conversation among cruisers — where are you from, where have you been, where are you going next. Lise and Dave were Australian and were on year two of a Pacific tour. Last season they'd left *Wildflower* in Tahiti and flown back to Brisbane for six months. They'd only returned to the boat recently.

"I thought it would be hard to get back into the cruising mindframe," Lise said, "but nope. I can hardly even remember what it's like to work 9 to 5 anymore."

"That's because it's work 24/7," Dave said, laughing. "We still haven't got the baby stay up yet, but I wasn't willing to hang around the yard any more. There's no such thing as being a hundred percent ready so bugger it! We'll be fixing things on the move no matter what, so I said let's just go and here we are."

"So, what's your deal?" Lise finally asked once we were on to our second round of drinks. Mat explained the company and our bizarre mission to just keep moving.

"That's awesome," Lise said. "What a great way for you guys to work and cruise at the same time."

"We've met a few big fancy yachts with crew," Dave said. "Never seen the owners but the crew can party with the best of them. But of course never on the the boat they're on — it's incredible to watch them polishing this and waxing that all day every day. I guess that's why it's a job."

"That's not how we are on *Byte Bucket*," Isaac said. "It's work, and there's stuff we have to do, but it reminds me more of family cruising than professional crew."

"My first job was on one of those megayachts," Tulia said. "You get to travel and it can be lots of fun at times, but it's hard work. This is a lot more laid-back."

"I'm obviously not working you lot hard enough," Mat said with a scowl, but there was a laugh in her voice. She caught Tulia's gaze out the corner of her eye and added, "Maybe you'll all have to pick up some slack in a bit."

Dave and Lise just laughed, but the rest of us knew what she meant. None of us wanted to think about what it would be like if Tulia left us at Mo'orea, but we all knew that it was a very real possibility.

We chatted a little longer and finished our drinks, but what Mat said brought us all down a little and we made our excuses soon thereafter. We'd consumed enough that we managed to pack all of us into the dinghy and Isaac slowly motored us back to the *Bucket*, where Christine and I helped Jimmy stow the few leftovers. Everyone was in bed by the time I rolled into my bunk except Martin and Tulia who were talking quietly on the foredeck.

I dreamed of Jeannette breaking up with me again, for my own good. "I don't want to hold you back," she said, "so I'm not going to." In my dream she was here with me, and we talked on the foredeck of the *Bucket*, then she jumped overboard when she said she was leaving. I watched her swim away, saw her become a lithe dolphin darting through the waves. When she jumped out of the water with a little flip it was as if she was telling me to find my own sense of freedom. But it didn't feel like freedom. It felt like something dying.

We stayed another night at Hanamoenoa, then sailed up to Nuku Hiva. It was only a day trip and I enjoyed the luxury of being at anchor every night. After lunch, I went down to the server room to check on things. The system was running well enough but there was a message from headquarters. I downloaded the header to see if it was small enough to grab from the satellites and was glad I had — the message was huge. Like megabytes huge.

In normal land life, a 20 MB attachment would be no big deal. But over the satellite connection it would take ages to come down plus eat up bandwidth that we were currently using for clients' data. I hesitated over clicking the download link.

The irony of the situation didn't escape me. We were a cloud data service — pushing other people's bytes around was what we did — and here I was, stressing about a twenty-meg download. But I felt like I had to prioritize the limited bandwidth for the clients. We were still running hot, and while a short slowdown wouldn't kill the system, I also figured that there wasn't anything in the email that couldn't wait until we anchored. Jimmy had explained that we were headed for the most populated town in the Marquesas, so I was pretty confident that we'd tap into the cell network when we get closer. I decided to wait.

I was curious, though. What could they be sending

me?

⚓

We pulled into Taiohae bay in the late afternoon. I wasn't sure what I expected, but it wasn't the wide open bay with room for many boats to anchor. I'd just imagined that everything here would be small and tight, like Atuona or even Hanamoenoa, but Taiohae reminded me more of Costa Rica. I couldn't even count the boats at anchor and we found a spot easily with lots of room between us and our nearest neighbour.

Jimmy got dinner underway and I went back down to the server room. The connection had automatically switched over to the cell network and traffic speed was up. I queued up the email to download and checked over the logs while I waited for it to arrive. Even on the faster network, it wasn't going to be immediate.

"Hey." I jumped at Martin's voice. I hadn't heard him come down the ladder and it took a moment for my heart to get back into my chest.

"Jeez! Creep around much?"

"Sorry. Uh, you have a sec?"

I shrugged. "Sure." I waited, but he didn't say anything, just looked at his feet as if there were something desperately interesting going on down there. There wasn't.

"Tulia, right?" I said, tired of waiting.

"Yeah."

I took a deep breath and let it out slowly. "There isn't anything any of us can do. It's between her and her family and she has to do what's right for her. Sometimes the right thing isn't the same as the thing you want. A job probably isn't worth alienating her whole family."

"But —"

I interrupted his protests. "I'm not saying it would come to that; I don't know anything you don't know. But sometimes we all have to do stuff that we don't want to do. It's just life."

He looked at me, a miserable look on his face. "It's not just a job," he said finally, so quiet I almost didn't hear it.

"I know," I said. "But still."

"Yeah."

"According to Isaac we're at least a week away from Mo'orea."

"A week. That's just great."

"It's better than nothing. And do you want to spend that week moping around down here with me or hanging out with her?"

He scowled at me but said "yeah" and turned to climb up the ladder. "Thanks," he muttered halfway up, then disappeared.

I understood how he felt perfectly well, but I also knew that if Tulia did end up leaving the boat he'd hate himself later if he wasted this time.

The email had downloaded by now, so I tried to refocus on work and opened it up. It was a mass message to all the remote admins advising us of a new node that had been brought online in the wake of all the new customers. I shouldn't have been surprised — more money plus more traffic made a pretty good business case for more infrastructure. The big attachment was a set of configuration tools to sync up with the new servers. It was meant to be as simple as possible, but I knew it would take a bit of time to get everything set up correctly and I could smell something suspiciously like burgers on the grill.

It would have to wait until tomorrow. My stomach was rumbling and I was ready for dinner. I made sure to save the config program locally then shut everything down and went up above decks. We all found space in the cockpit and aft deck with grilled burgers on baguettes. I saw Martin and Tulia together, laughing and talking, and I smiled a bit sadly to myself. *T'is better to have loved and lost* and all that, right?

Yeah, right.

⚓

I woke early the next morning and got the new network configuration up and running before most of the crew were even awake. I'd given up all pretence of following an orderly schedule and worked when it was convenient, slept when I was tired and let everything else just kind of happen. There were times when I found it hard to believe that I was living like that — I'd always been a devotee of the colour-coded calendar — but when in Rome. Or, as it happened, Taiohae.

I was slotting my freshly washed breakfast dishes into the clever wooden housings in the galley when a sleepy-eyed Mat walked into the mess. "Morning," she grunted at me, not uncheerfully.

"Is it still morning?"

"Har har." She drew a cup of coffee and opened the pantry. "How's your magic box of smoke and mirrors?"

"Sailing full and by, Cap'n." She froze with her coffee cup halfway to her mouth and blinked at me slowly. "That *is* boat talk for everything's all right, isn't it?"

I was almost sure that I saw a grin behind her cup, but she took a sip and swallowed before answering. "Yeah," she admitted, "more or less." She poured a bowl of cereal and poked in the fridge for the box of milk. "You busy down in the bilge today?"

I shook my head. "I took care of everything for today already."

She looked at me incredulously, then said, "Can I ask a favour, then?"

"Sure."

"You willing to help me haul the number 2 ashore? There's a sail loft and I want to see what outrageous price they'll charge to stitch up a couple of seams. I can do it myself but it's way easier with two."

"Okay."

My confusion must have come through in my voice, because she said, "Isaac's busy with Christine on some engine thing, and Jimmy's going to have his hands full with provisions." She paused for a bite of cereal, then nonchalantly added, "The others have the day off."

"Gotcha," I said, and turned away so she couldn't

see my smile. In all the time I'd been aboard it had never seemed like we had "days off" as such, but Mat was obviously as much of a romantic as I was. Besides, this was the first time she asked me to participate in any of the boat work and it felt great.

She told me to meet above decks in half an hour ready to go ashore, so I went back to my bunk to get organized.

⚓

I couldn't imagine that the sail piled up on deck like a giant soft-serve ice cream could possibly fit in the bag that Mat held in her hands. "Just do what I tell you," she said, "and be careful dragging the sailcloth — we don't want any more tears."

A chill of fear ran through me. I thought I was volunteering for the grunt work of carrying a bulky object, not anything delicate.

"Just lift it at that end to keep it off the deck a little while I stretch it out." I gulped and grabbed the edge of the sailcloth. It was heavy, a lot heavier than I expected, but I lifted it up around the level of my knees while Mat lifted and pulled the other sides back. Pretty soon the sail was laid out over the whole foredeck and Mat started to fold it in on itself. Following her directions, we folded it like a giant flag, until it was a long rectangle. Then she picked up one end and began folding it down until it was a bundle about the size of a large duffel bag.

"Hold that open for me," she said, pointing at the sailbag, and I saw that it was clearly going to fit after all.

She wrestled the bundle into the bag and pulled its drawstring cord closed. "Grab one end and let's get this into the dinghy."

It was heavy, but she was right that between the two of us it wasn't that hard to carry. We got to the transom and carefully maneuvered it on to the swim step, then Mat got into the dinghy and I helped her haul it in. She climbed out again and gave me an appraising look. "Thanks," she said. "We'll be going ashore as soon as everyone else is ready." At that she walked into the main salon and shouted "Shore leave!" in the direction of the companionway. She turned at me and grinned. "Shouldn't be long now."

She was right. Like cats responding to the sound of a can opener the entire crew, even Isaac and Christine, came out to the cockpit. "I don't want to start the oil change until you guys are gone," Christine explained. "It's fiddly work and a lot easier with some space to breathe."

The rest of us loaded into the dinghy, Jimmy with a set of empty bags that I expected to be full of food for the return trip, Martin and Tulia carefully not looking at each other. We pulled up to a rusty ladder along a concrete wall and I looked at Mat with an eyebrow raised. "We came ashore at high water for a reason," she said. Turning to the three others, she said, "You bunch go first, then Devi and I will pass the sail up to you. I really do not want it to end up in the drink, got it?" There were nods all around, and the three of them climbed up one by one. Mat and I carefully held up the sail bag to them. I was scared of standing up in the dinghy without hanging on to anything, but I braced my feet wide apart and discovered that it wasn't that tough to stand on my own. We stretched up and soon hands from above had grabbed the bag and pulled it up on to the dock.

"No chance that would have worked in a southerly," Mat said and I nodded as if I understood, then climbed up the ladder myself. Mat followed, hanging on to the dinghy's line. She pulled the boat along the edge until it was out of the way of the ladder and in a more secure location with several other dinghies. She tied it off and then walked back to the rest of us. "Two hours?" She said it as if it were a question, but I doubted anyone would have thought to say no. There were some glances at phones and watches, then Jimmy went off toward the shops and Martin and Tulia walked into a nearby park.

"Grab an end," Mat said and I complied before we walked to a nearby building next to an area that looked like it was used as a public market or meeting place but was deserted now. We wrestled the sail bag through an open doorway and into a large space that was made infinitely smaller by the crowding of sails, flags, rope ends, mysterious hardware and a million odds and ends I couldn't come close to identifying.

"'Allo?" Mat called and a muffled answer came from above. Hot pink Croc-clad feet appeared at the top of a steep staircase, followed by a woman of indeterminate age wearing some kind of tie-dyed kaftan contraption in greens and blues with a voluminous pair of faded orange harem pants.

I'd grown accustomed to Mat's backpacker-hippie outfits — today she was wearing a pair of men's jeans that were more holes than denim and a faded yellow tee-shirt under what was certainly meant to be a sundress. It was one of her more normal outfits and in comparison to the person she was now negotiating with in rapid-fire French, it actually did appear normal.

My French wasn't up to following their conversation, so I looked around the room. I got the impression that this was mainly a repair and restock kind of place. There were tapes and needles, kits labelled in English for repairing tears and reinforcing edges, a few flags for what I assumed were islands in the South Pacific. We'd raised the *Trois Couleurs* when we cleared in at Hiva Oa along with another very pretty flag depicting a stylized sailboat that Isaac told me was the flag of French Polynesia, and there were a few of each of those available for sale here as well.

I'd picked up an ancient-looking wood and metal pulley and was examining its simple mechanism when I was startled by hearing English. "You think we need a new block and tackle?" Mat had obviously finished with the sailmaker and had somehow crept up behind me. I nearly dropped the heavy object but fumbled it back on to its shelf.

"Sorry—"

"I love these old wooden blocks," Mat said as if nothing untoward had occurred. "Classic timber yachts are a real pleasure, both to look at and to sail. But the maintenance is unbelievable. I don't think you could pay me to own one. But it's great that some people are willing to put in the effort." She ran a finger over the gleaming varnished wood of some other piece of equipment nearby then said, "Come on."

We walked out of the shop and continued on toward town. "Madame's going to need a few days with the genny, so we won't go far until it's ready. There are some nice bays on this island, though. I think we'll spent another night here and maybe move around tomorrow afternoon."

"You don't like staying in one spot very long?" I immediately regretting saying it — it sounded like an accusation and that wasn't what I'd meant at all. Mat didn't seem to mind, though.

"Not really. That's part of how I ended up sailing. I love arriving somewhere new, but after a while I get... I don't know—" She looked off into the distance as if she would find the right word in a copse of palm trees. "*Itchy* is the only word I can think of that feels right." She shrugged. "That's why this job works so well for me. They like it if we keep on the move. Something about making it hard to trace something something?"

I chuckled. "Yeah, that sounds right."

She glanced at her watch. "We have about an hour. I might see if Jimmy needs some help picking the good stuff. You okay on your own? Want to come along?"

Grocery shopping didn't really appeal and I had

secretly hoped that I'd get a few minutes with some café's wifi so I could send off some emails home.

"I'm good by myself, thanks. Meet you back at the wharf?"

"Yup." She looked me over and smiled, just slightly. "Thanks for the help today, by the way. You know you don't have to, but I've noticed you pitching in. I appreciate it."

I mumbled something about it being nothing, then made my escape. I don't know why her acknowledgement meant so much to me, but it felt like getting an A+ report card from Miss Patel in Grade Three.

⚓

I spent a while walking up and down the main street of Taiohae. It was much larger than Atuona, but there were still only a handful of cafes. A few had the magical lure of the wifi symbol on the door and I finally chose one that didn't look like they'd mind if I just had a coffee and a croissant while I surfed.

I managed to make my order in my bad French, then sat by myself in a corner at a table for two. I connect to their network and waited as my phone picked up my emails. I was surprised at how few there were. I'd been offline for almost a month, but there were only a couple from my dad, one from my brother and the rest were newsletters, updates or the other not-quite-spam that fill inboxes the world over. I just deleted those unread.

The oldest email from my dad was actually from both mom and dad, a short newsy message about my cousin Trina's engagement. I didn't know her well and probably wouldn't even be invited to the wedding, but it was family news. The next message opened with dad saying that he had forgotten how long I was going to be offline and that he hoped everything was okay, then became the kind of message I was accustomed to from him.

He'd always been a yakker — even when I was a kid, he'd spend most days after work talking to me about whatever had gone on that day, not expecting any response or even making sense half the time. He just needed an outlet and I was always willing to listen. When I'd moved out, he'd continued the tradition by sending me periodic emails that often referenced people I'd never heard of or told half stories that didn't go anywhere. It was like he was keeping a journal, just in the form of emails he sent me.

It was odd, but I found them comforting. It wasn't a conversation, really. It was more like the kind of venting you do with friends over a drink, where you don't need them to offer a solution or even understand, just get it out. I loved that Dad still did that with me, that he still saw me as his sounding board even though I was half a world away. I was grinning when the cute, tattooed young woman working at the cafe brought my order over, and she smiled back at me. "Merci," I said, understanding a little bit about those sailors who had a girl in every port.

I was still thinking about the waitress when opened the message from Nico, but all thoughts of her were soon lost. I knew from his opening line that this wasn't going to be good:

```
Everything is okay and don't panic.

Mom and dad said they didn't want
to worry you so they aren't going
to tell you but that doesn't seem
right and I think you'd want to
know. Grandma is in the hospital.
They don't know what's wrong, but
she was in the supermarket the
other day and her legs just gave
out. Grandad was there and he got
her to the emergency room and they
admitted her right away.

She's telling everyone that she's
fine she's walking around a little
better now but the doctors still
haven't figured out why she lost
control in the first place. There
was talk that she maybe had a
stroke.

Mom is at the hospital everyday and
says she's getting better, but who
knows, she'd old, right? Anyway, I
thought you should know, just in
case.

Love,
N
```

I could feel that sharp pain in my sinuses that I got when tears were about to start welling up in my eyes. I took a deep breath to try and make them stop and blinked a few times. Nico had said that Grandma was more or less fine, but still. What if? There was no way I could get home in time if...

I looked down at my half-eaten croissant. I couldn't

finish it now. I fired off a quick email to Nico asking for an update then paid my bill. The waitress looked at me as if as she wanted to ask if I was okay, but I didn't want to have that conversation in any language, so just handed her some bills. At the last minute I remembered what Tulia had told me about tipping being borderline offensive here and pocketed my change, then walked out into the brightness outside. I had a few minutes to walk off the dread I was feeling as I made my way back to the dinghy.

Chapter Nine

Last Stop Until Tahiti

I couldn't stop thinking about that email I'd gotten from my brother — don't panic, but your grandmother is in the hospital and can't really walk. I wanted to talk about it with someone, but Martin and Tulia were both wrapped up in each other and no one else seemed right. Christine and Isaac were swearing and covered in black engine oil when we got back to the *Bucket* and I knew that talking to either of them about anything would have been a recipe for disaster. Jimmy was, well, Jimmy. The idea of talking to him about being worried about my grandma made me feel like a little kid, which I didn't want right now. It was bad enough being half way around the world from them without essentially saying "I miss my mommy and daddy" out loud. And Mat was completely out. I hadn't felt so alone since the first day I came aboard.

I'd sent Nico a message back, but I wasn't going to get his answer until I got ashore again for another hit of wifi. I tried not to think about it, but the image of my grandmother just losing control in a supermarket kept running through my head. She wasn't a large woman — even I was taller than her — but she was formidable. It hadn't been easy for her and Grandad to come to Canada from India, especially since they weren't religious, so a lot of the community and cultural connections that they might have had as new immigrants were lost to them. But they had made a life for themselves, raising my mom and my uncles, and becoming successful business-owners. Grandma was who I always looked up to when I'd had a hard time. When I came out, she was the first person I told. I loved her and didn't want to think that anything could happen to her.

So, when Mat told us all at dinner that she was going to move the boat to a little bay on the north side of the island, I nearly lost it. I was taking a breath to argue with her when Christine beat me to the punch.

"No, you're not," she said and Mat just looked at her. "Not unless I get several litres of oil in the engine."

Mat blinked a couple of times, and I wondered what she was going to say. I'd never heard anyone actually contradict her before. Finally she just nodded.

"Okay. Go ashore first thing in the morning and get the engine oil. Hopefully, you can get us going and we'll head out in the afternoon." Then she went back to her dinner as if nothing had happened.

I helped Jimmy clean up after the meal, as I often did now. Martin and Tulia were off together and once the last dish was put away I went in search of Christine. We had never been particularly friendly but in the last few weeks we'd reached a kind of détente. I had to at least ask.

"Hey," I said, interrupting her reading. She nodded at me, then put her book down. "So, do you have to go into town tomorrow?"

She nodded. "We had to flush the engine today, and we used the last of our good oil so I need to get more.

Why?"

I took a breath. "I was hoping I could come with you and maybe have a minute at one of the internet cafés."

"I'm not planning on being very long," she said, frowning.

"I can be fast."

She looked at me funny. "Is everything okay?"

I really hadn't planned on talking to her about this. I just wanted a lift ashore, but it all came out in a jumble.

"It's my grandmother. She fell and now she's in the hospital. Nico said that she's going to be fine and my parents didn't even tell me, but it's driving me crazy not knowing. I just want to get an update from my brother, that's all."

I blinked the tears out of my eyes and took a breath. Christine didn't say anything for a moment, then picked up her book, putting her bookmark in and setting it aside.

"This is the worst part," she said. "Being out here, travelling, it's great and I love it but sometimes stuff happens back in the real world and you just can't do anything about it. It sucks, I know. My Uncle Ross died when I was on one of my first passages and I didn't even find out until after the funeral. It was an accident — hit by a drunk driver — so when I learned about it I couldn't even believe it. It was like one day he was there and the next..." She snapped her fingers. "I still forget sometimes. Someone will say something he'd have said and I think,

'I've got to tell Ross...' and then—" She looked away. "Anyway, I understand. Let's go ashore first thing tomorrow morning, get breakfast and you can check your messages, then you can help me carry the oil back, okay?"

I felt something heavy in my chest and didn't really trust myself to talk. "Thanks," I more or less whispered, then walked down to my bunk.

⚓

Isaac was the only one up when Christine and I left the next morning and he gave us a confused look and opened his mouth to say something, but let it go when she gave her head a little shake. We loaded into the dinghy and walked into town before anyone else had gotten off the boats. There was a little snack next to the small chandlery and we went in, ordering coffees and croissants.

"Go ahead," Christine said and I fired up my phone. It took forever to connect to the café's wireless, but eventually I did and loaded my email. Nico had answered and I had a moment of fear as my finger hovered over the message. I tapped it and held my breath.

```
Hey. Sorry to worry you, but I
really thought you'd want to know.
Grandma's doing much better now,
walking and everything. They've
given her one of those four-point
canes and they're going to release
her tomorrow, probably because
she's making life miserable for the
nurses. They still don't know what
caused it in the first place,
though, which is worrying. Mom
isn't taking it well, honestly, but
what can you do? She nearly got
```

```
into it with the doctors the other
day and dad had to practically drag
her away.

No one blames you for not being
here. I showed your message to
Grandma and she laughed — she told
me to tell you not to worry about
her and that you need to live your
own life. She said she'd come over
there and remind you if she had to,
you know what she's like.

Anyway, it's okay here. Mom is a
bit crazy and Grandma isn't 100%
but I think it's all going to be
fine. Really. Don't worry.

Love,
N
```

I let out a breath I hadn't known I'd been holding, and Christine looked up. She didn't say anything, but I could see the question in her eyes. "She's okay," I said but I couldn't get anything else out after that.

She grinned at me and said, "I'm really glad to her that. So, you going to eat that?" I looked down at my untouched croissant and grinned.

"Yeah, actually, I think I am."

⚓

I began to wonder if Christine's bargain of letting me come ashore in exchange for help carrying was particularly altruistic after all. Each backpack held only two large bottles and they were like carrying cement. The walk back to the wharf felt like it took twice as long. By now, a few other dinghies had joined ours and an older lady with a strong accent helped us get aboard with our awkward cargo. Even with the breakfast stop and the slow walk back to the wharf, we still got back to the *Bucket* before Mat was awake.

Christine disappeared into the engine room with the backpacks and I went down to the server room for my daily check. The new configuration was running like a champ and everything looked good in the logs. Traffic was up again and I felt a blush of weird pride that the company seemed to be doing well. I knew that my contributions weren't really making that much of an impact in terms of getting new users, but it still felt good to be part of something that was taking off. I wondered if this was kind of what it felt like to be involved in a start-up that went viral. It was cool.

I heard — and felt — the engine start up as I was poking through the traffic logs. I ignored it at first, since Christine was working on it and I knew you had to start them up when you were doing things. At least, our neighbour Jan used to do that when she was fiddling with her old Firebird first thing in the morning on Saturdays when I was a kid. *Engines — they need to run.*

I'd let the sound and vibration fade into the background, when I felt a lurch and heard the grinding on the windlass. Mat hadn't been kidding about wanting to move on. I shut everything down, making sure that the network connection was going to switch over, then made my way up above decks. By the time I got to the cockpit, the anchor was up and we were motoring out of the harbour.

The sail around the east coast of the island up to Anahoe Bay was uneventful, which I knew now was how I liked it. There were a few other cruising boats moving around and Jimmy brought sandwich fixings and fruit juice up once the main was raised and the smaller foresail that we still had aboard unfurled. It was a leisurely and pleasant sail, and I spent the whole time up in the cockpit looking at the tall, jagged cliffs of Nuku Hiva.

Anahoe Bay was crowded as Taiohae had been when we turned the corner in the late afternoon. There was space for us near the entrance, though, and soon the anchor was down and Isaac started setting up the hammocks. I'd actually forgotten that we had them.

"I am dying for a swim." Christine passed me on the way down to the bunks.

"Great idea," I said, following her to get my suit. A few minutes later I was headfirst off the side of the boat, the warm water washing sweat and worries off me. I did a couple of laps around the boat, noticing a few patches of green slime on the bottom. I pulled myself up on to the swim step at the back of the boat and rummaged around in the locker back there. I found a scraper, and looped its lanyard over my wrist, then let myself slide back into the water. I spent maybe ten minutes taking care of the bits of growth I found, then decided it was time to get out anyway. I pulled myself up to the swim step and nearly had a heart attack when I found Isaac's face peering down at me.

"Jeez!"

"Sorry," he said, then looked at the scraper hanging from my arm. "Uh..."

"Oh," I said, pulling it off and stowing it in the locker. "I just thought I'd take care of it, since I was down there anyway."

He looked at me and there was something funny in his face. He nodded and said, "thanks," then disappeared. I shrugged and pulled out the freshwater hose that was kept in the aft locker. I let a short blast loose over my head and washed the saltwater off, then turned it off and put it away. There was no one in the hammocks so I just let myself drip-dry in the sun until Jimmy called us all for food.

It was hard to believe that just that morning I'd been freaking out over being here. Honestly, it was kind of hard to believe that I was here at all.

⚓

After dinner, Mat declared rum rations, so a big cooler full of beer was brought up on deck, along with some juice and cans of Coke I didn't even know we had. And the rum, of course.

Christine handed me a large plastic tumbler of rum and juice, and clicked her own glass with mine. "We deserve these after the last couple of days." I grinned at her and nodded, taking a sip. She'd mixed them strong.

"That oil change blew," Isaac said, popping open a beer, "but what's your story? Something go crazy with the servers again?"

"It's a personal thing," Christine said before I could get a word in, her voice taking a tone that strongly indicated that Isaac should shut the hell up. "It's none of your business."

Isaac's eyes widened and I thought he was going to try to slink away, so I said, "It's okay, Christine. Thanks for trying to keep it private but I'm fine now." I turned to Isaac. "My grandmother had a health scare and I wasn't sure what was going on. I found out this morning that she's okay, but it was a tough time."

"Oh, yeah" he said, nodding. "That's the worst. I'm glad she's going to be all right."

"Thanks." We watched the sun go down behind the hills, turning the sky a lurid orange and pink. "How do you manage it?" I said after a while.

"Being cut off from family?"

"It's not just family," Isaac said. "It's kind of everything."

"Yeah," I said, looking back and forth between them. "That."

Isaac shrugged. "It's not all bad. Not knowing every little thing that goes on the world is pretty liberating. But, yeah, it can suck, too. Even with all our social life, the radio nets and satellite email, we're essentially still alone out here. Stuff happens out there," he gestured out to sea, "and you can't do anything about it. It can feel pretty lonely."

"Yeah," Christine said, "but you usually can't do anything about that kind of stuff no matter where you are. I mean, Devi, if you were home now, could you have done anything to help your grandma? Would you really have worried any less?"

I thought about it for a second. "Probably not," I admitted. "But at least I could have seen her."

Both of them just nodded at that. I knew Christine was thinking of her uncle and I guessed that Isaac had one or two memories come back to him, too.

⚓

We each had a few refills and soon the conversation became a bit less maudlin. Martin and Tulia had gone ashore for a "walk" but they joined the group after returning. I'd never seen Martin drink like he did that night — it was as if he were putting in a heroic effort to get drunk, and unsurprisingly it worked. It wasn't bad; he was actually pretty funny with half a dozen beers in him, but I could see that he was already mourning the end of his relationship with Tulia. I wondered if she'd made up her mind and that's what they'd been talking about all those times they took off together. I hoped it was something else, at least some of the time.

He ended up going to bed before any of the rest of us, and I found myself up in the hammocks on the foredeck with Tulia looking at the stars.

"Poor Martin," she said. "He is going to have a rough morning."

"Yeah," I laughed.

"He's taking it well, considering," she said after a moment. My heart dropped. I thought she might have made a decision, and I'd known for longer than anyone else that this might be happening, but until that moment I'd never really thought she'd leave the boat.

"You're going ashore?"

"What choice do I have? My brother has offered me a job that pays more than I can get being a deckhand, even if I went back to working on a megayacht. My parents hate that I'm out here on my own, and it's not like there's anything for me here to justify making them all miserable. I've had my little adventure, I'm not a kid anymore. It's time to grow up."

I didn't say anything for a moment. It sounded a lot like the kind of thing that I would say without even a hint of the bittersweet part. Or maybe it was the kind of thing I would have said a few months ago. Now, though...

"And Martin?"

"Poor Martin," she repeated. She didn't have to tell me that this wasn't one of those love will conquer all kinds of things. It was the adult equivalent of a summer romance — fun and intense and temporary. They both knew that. I doubted that made it not hurt, though.

⚓

Martin survived the next day, if only barely. We stayed another night at Anahoe, me, Isaac and Christine joining a group of three other boats on a massive hike along the ridge that took most of the afternoon. The views were amazing — there is something strangely magical about looking down into a bay where the boat you're staying on is anchored. That evening was subdued and we were underway the next morning fairly early. Mat decided to take the long way around the island back to Taiohae, so it was a full day getting back.

The next morning I helped Jimmy with another load of food. He'd gotten up before five am to get to the bakery in town, and he'd been ashore and come back once before I even got up. "They're closed by seven," he explained, which I wouldn't have believed if anyone else had said it. He wasn't usually an early riser.

Isaac and Mat picked up the sail while we were at the market and the dinghy was packed on the return trip. It took forever to unload everything, but we made it and I helped Jimmy stow what seemed like enough food for another ocean passage.

"Where are we going?" I asked. "Africa?"

He laughed. "Naw, we're stopping at the Tuomotos before we get to Tahiti. They're amazing — reef lagoons. The snorkelling is unbelievable. But there isn't a lot there, so this is pretty much the last stop for food until Tahiti."

"Ah." That explained it.

The last stop until Tahiti. The thought made me sad and I couldn't help but think, "Poor Martin."

It was nearly a week to get to Fakarava, our first stop in the Tuomotos, and it was not a particularly comfortable one. I'd thought I'd gotten my sea legs on the long ocean passage, but the first day out of Nuku Hiva I felt like I'd never been on a boat before. I even got that strange half-queasy feeling in my stomach and could barely eat anything.

I tried to keep out of everyone's way — I felt pretty useless and moving around a lot didn't strike me as a particularly good idea. I parked myself in the main salon, more or less in the same place as I'd lived while my ribs were healing, and tried to read. It wasn't great.

Tulia came through on her way down below and flopped into the seat beside me.

"Gotta say, this is making me feel pretty good about getting off the boat."

"Yeah," I said. "I'm not used to it anymore, either."

She shook her head. "This is unusually rough. The swells are big and we're rocking and rolling like crazy. I don't really know why we didn't wait for it to die down, but Mat has her reasons, I'm sure."

Isaac happened to walk up the companionway at that moment and laughed. "Sometimes I wonder, but this time she does, yeah." Tulia looked chagrined and started to say something, but Isaac just went on. "It's shitty right now, but by the time we get to the pass the swell should have died down. If we were there right now, we wouldn't even get in."

"The what?"

"The pass," Tulia explained. "Fakarava is a ring reef, and to get into the lagoon you have to cross a part of the reef that's deeper under water than the rest of it — that's the pass. It can be pretty dangerous if there's big sea running."

"Yeah, like impassable," Isaac said. "So Mat's plan is that we suffer now, but the seas should reduce over the next few days, making it a better passage every day. And by the time we arrive, getting through the pass should be a piece of cake."

"Oh." And I'd thought I was getting the hang of this sailing thing.

⚓

Isaac was right — it did get better. The first night I slept terribly; I wasn't certain that by the time I got up the next day that I'd ever actually been asleep. I don't know if I was just getting used to the motion or if the waves did get smaller, but by the time the sun went down on the second night I felt a lot more comfortable. Maybe getting a decent meal helped, too, but that night I slept well. By the morning of Day Three I felt like I had near the end of the long ocean passage and was able to enjoy the ride.

The water was an amazing turquoise colour that I was certain I'd never seen before, and since there were many islands in the area there was a lot more marine life. Mat gave up putting the line out after she'd caught two tuna, and we were shadowed by birds almost the entire trip.

"I know this should be boring," I said to Christine one afternoon, sitting in the cockpit and looking out at the seemingly endless expanse of ocean around us, "but I feel like I could watch the water go by all day long."

"It's always the same and always different," she said. "That's kind of what I love about being out here."

I nodded and let myself drift off in my mind while I watched the big blue do its thing.

⚓

We got to the pass at Fakarava around midday, which apparently was due to some careful planning on Mat's part. "You want to have the sun as high as possible, because we have to navigate by sight on the way in." I assumed she was kidding. I'd watched us navigate through small channels and around rocks by the GPS and electronic charts up on the large screen in the cockpit. Here, though, that wasn't going to cut it.

"These passes aren't charted," Isaac explained, "not really. And of course, coral grows, so they change anyway. You have to just look."

And look is exactly what they did.

Isaac got into his harness and climbed halfway up the mainmast while Mat took the wheel. They'd dowsed the sails and were running the engine and I understood why Christine was so concerned about making sure it was in top order before we left.

We motored slowly in toward the pass, and even I

could tell that we were in the right place — waves were crashing into sprays of white on either side of the area of clear water that we were aiming at. It was nerve-wracking and everyone was silent except for Isaac who shouted *port* and *starboard* when he wanted us to turn.

It felt like it took forever and as we passed between the breaking waves I looked overboard and saw the bottom of the sea as clearly as if there were nothing but air between us. It was disorienting, and I couldn't tell how far down the bottom was, but obviously it was deeper than our draft as we made it into the lagoon without any issues. Isaac came down from the mast as we puttered into the anchorage.

⚓

The water was warm as a bath as I lazily floated on the surface. Jimmy was right about the snorkelling — the views under the water here were spectacular. It was partly because the sheltered lagoon was excellent for marine animals and partly because it was so remote that there weren't many people. It felt like flying though a magical garden at times, the colourful corals making homes for what seemed like a million different fish. Tiny yellow and blue striped fish swam among large parrotfish, huge groups of dinner-plate size snapper cruised by, and I even saw a clownfish nestled in an anemone.

Almost the whole crew had gone swimming together — only Isaac and Jimmy stayed aboard — and we were prowling over the coral heads in an area Mat knew about. We'd taken the dinghy over, Christine diving down with a line and tying it to a dead piece of coral as an anchor. We then swam around the large reef, with its whole universe of life. I was totally engrossed in watching a small blue and yellow fish nibbling on some kind plant when something caught my eye. I swam around to see what it was when my heart stopped.

It was a fucking shark. No, that's not accurate. It was lots of fucking sharks. Like, maybe eight.

Something in my brain must have kicked in, because my immediate reaction to flail around and try to get away was tamped down and I forced myself to pop up and look around for the rest of the group. We were all fairly close together, so I slowly swam over to the others. I found Tulia first and popped my snorkel out of my mouth.

"Shark." I croaked out, half whispering as if saying it out loud would prompt some kind of Jaws-like scenario.

"I know!" She grinned. "Aren't they awesome?"

"Um," I looked at her, baffled. "No. They're fucking sharks!"

"Oh." A look of understanding crossed her face. "They're reef sharks; totally harmless. They're scared of *you*. If you get too close to them, they'll just swim away."

"But..." I didn't know how to explain myself. "Sharks?"

"If you're freaked out, just get in the dinghy. We're probably going to go soon anyway. But really, they're fine. I'll come with you if you want."

Tulia was a lot of things, but reckless wasn't one of

them. It must have been that same, sensible, logical part of my brain that stopped me from panicking earlier that said, "Okay. Maybe just for a sec." We put our snorkels back in and I followed just behind Tulia as we swam back to where the sharks were. Now, I noticed that they were quite small, each one maybe just a bit longer than my arm, and they were skittish. When a little fish darted out from behind a piece of coral, the sharks near to it turned around and swam off. Now that I really watched them, they didn't seem so scary after all.

Pretty soon they'd all swum away and we returned to the dinghy. Tulia and I hauled ourselves in and took off our masks and flippers. Soon, Martin and Mat joined us, and like a five-year-old I couldn't stop myself from boasting, "I swam with sharks!"

They didn't laugh at me, though, and as we motored our way back to the Bucket I thought to myself that I wasn't living a life of quiet desperation. And no matter what happened to me in the rest of my life, I could say, "Whatever. I swam with fucking sharks."

⚓

That night we held a huge party, inviting all the other cruisers in the anchorage. Jimmy's monster provisioning trip made even more sense in that context. There were people everywhere — the main salon was packed, there were folks hanging out down below, several groups on the foredeck and cockpit. It was intense and fun. I took a bunch of groups on tours of the boat — everyone was curious about the layout compared to their smaller boats.

The crowd thinned out as the evening wore on, and soon most of us were in the cockpit with some spillover on the aft deck. The conversation had turned around to how we all ended up out here. Most of the cruisers were retirees on their dream trip, but there was one obviously younger couple — Inez, one of the few Latinas I'd met among the other boats, and her partner, Mark. I could tell that many of the older folks wondered how they could afford to be out here with no job or other visible means of support. Eventually one of the grandpas just gave up all pretence.

"So, are y'all dotcom millionaires or somethin'?"

Inez laughed and shook her head. "That's actually a bit before my time. And not likely. One," she ticked off points on her fingers, "neither of us can do much more than turn a computer on and two, we aren't millionaires. On our best day, we're thousandaires. We just saved a lot and are good at being frugal."

"Sounds hard," a lady off one of the other boats said.

"Yeah," Mark answered. "I guess. But everything is hard. And it's a lot nicer being broke out here than it would have been back in the States." There were a few nods, but I noticed some skeptical expressions among the crowd.

"What made you want to go sailing?" That was Martin.

"Aside from the fact that it's the only way to get places like this—" Inez said to several nods around the cockpit, "mostly I guess it was that we didn't want to be those people who spend their whole adult lives talking about what they'll do *one day*. All of us out here are the exceptions to the rule. Most people talk about stuff but never do it. I know tons of people who spent years getting the boat ready, are still spending years getting the boat ready and they'll never go anywhere."

"It's true," one of the other cruisers said. "And good on you two for not just letting life happen to you."

Mark shrugged. "Thanks, but even out here stuff still just happens. There's no escaping that. That's the thing I've learned most from this life: there is no escape, there is no pure freedom. Even at sea, a squall can come up, and now there's a gale from the wrong direction but you've got full sail up. You can drop your sails, heave-to, turn and run with it. But you can do your best and sometimes that shit can still flatten you. It's the same as living ashore — you can lose your job over nothing you did and then boom: no rent, now you're homeless. Maybe you can find a new job, get some help, find a friend to stay with until it works out, but maybe you're not so lucky."

"Well that's a depressing thought," Martin said.

"Kind of," Mark said, "but when that squall's coming and I think 'ugh, why me?' it helps remind me to be thankful for all the stuff I can control in my life. It reminds me to be thankful that I realized so early that I can control things at all, and that I'm so lucky to be able to be out here dealing with this squall in the first place."

Everyone was quiet, then Inez said, "Or at least that what he says after the wind and rain are over. In the middle of every squall we've ever been in, it's just pretty much just a whole lot of swearing." That broke the tension and there were laughs and the refilling of glasses.

I couldn't stop thinking about what Mark had said. It sounded a lot like those horrible motivational posters you see decorating cubicle walls, but it really hit me. At first I'd felt like this whole experience was happening to me, that I was just riding one of those big swells that shoves the boat around. But now things were a little different — I might not have really chosen to be here at first, but I had chosen to make friends, to learn about the boat, to take advantage of this opportunity.

I swam with fucking sharks and it was my choice.

⚓

We all slept in the next day, so it wasn't until the day after that we left Fakarava. We stopped in at Rangiroa, the most populous atoll in the Tuomotos — I couldn't help thinking about that statistic as I walked along the ring of land that surrounded the lagoon, seeing the few houses and people there. We only spent one night there, but we all got a couple of rounds of snorkelling in. I didn't see any sharks this time, alas.

The next morning the swell had come up a bit and getting out of the pass was much more exciting than I'd hoped. Isaac had saved our GPS track from when we'd come in, so we could at least just follow that on the way out, but the large swells were tossing the boat around and the white water crashing on either side of us freaked me out. I must have looked as scared as I felt, because Tulia suggested I go down below for a bit. "I think that would be worse," I said, my eyes enormous as we crashed down over a particularly large wave. She just nodded, gave my shoulder a squeeze, then went back to preparing to raise the main.

Once we were out, everything calmed down and we had a good overnighter to Tahiti. The mood aboard was subdued, though, as we all knew that Tulia was going to be leaving once we got there. She hadn't made any kind of formal announcement, but I could tell that she'd spoken to everyone, since we were all just a bit sad. Our last voyage together. It had that bittersweet flavour of melancholy that last times always seem to share.

I was surprised when we pulled up to the docks in front of downtown Pape'ete rather than anchoring in the lagoon off the airport. I'd never been at a dock before and it felt so strange to be essentially attached to shore. Mat went to have a meeting with the boat's agent to make sure everything was fine with our customs and immigration, but the rest of us hung around the boat even through we were free to go ashore if we wanted to. Everyone was waiting for Tulia to go; no one wanted to miss out on her last few minutes on board.

I think she'd finally had enough of the rest of us tiptoeing around her and just after lunch announced to no one in particular that she was going ashore but she'd be back later. We all acted like it was perfectly normal, but you could feel the tension in the air. Martin looked like he was going to cry and Jimmy found a pressing need to do something in the galley with the door closed.

I spent the afternoon in the server room, connecting to the local cell network and poking around in the log files. The traffic was up again and I made sure that the new configuration was up to handling it. It was close, but I assumed that whatever had prompted a new bunch of customers would peak soon and throughput would normalize in a day or two. It was all good, but I managed to find more reasons to stay down there. Eventually I heard footsteps on the passarelle, the plank of wood that we used to get from the boat to the dock. It didn't sound like Mat, though I don't know why I thought that. I mustn't have been the only one, as the whole crew just happened to be hanging out on deck when I got up there.

It was Tulia with her brother, Rainui, in his island-style business casual outfit that radiated success. "This is it," Martin said as if he were talking to himself and I found myself reaching over to squeeze his hand. He squeezed back and didn't let go.

"You've come for your stuff?" Christine said what was on all our minds.

Tulia took a breath and looked over at her brother. He smiled at her and nodded slightly.

"No," she said. "I'm staying on board, at least for now. I told Mat this morning, but asked her not to say anything since I hadn't talked to my family yet. I just had a long conversation with them, and I'm staying. Rainui's here to take a look at the boat."

We were all stunned, but kept our composure

enough to let them get through to the interior of the boat. We followed them around as Tulia gave her brother the tour, and I caught myself watching him closely to see what his reaction was. Finally, we all ended up in the cockpit, and Jimmy remembered to bring up some juice and snacks.

"This is a lovely boat," Rainui said in accented English. "I can see why Tu likes it here." He smiled at her. "I remember when I was in school and my friends all laughed at me when I said I was going to own a resort one day. Even my teachers thought it was silly." He had a very serious expression on his face, and I worried that he was going to try to bully Tulia into changing her mind. "But I know I will do what I have to do," he went on. "My business is very important to me and I have worked hard to succeed." He turned to Tulia. "A good part of the work I have done is convincing people that I knew what I wanted, that I could do it. I am sorry I didn't understand that this is what you were doing, too."

They both beamed at each other, and I was pretty sure I heard someone behind me choking back a sob. Luckily, Mat saved us from making some kind of emotional scene by coming up the passarelle.

"Ah, Monsieur Laille, bonjour. Bienvenue au *Byte Bucket*." She and Rainui had a brief conversation in rapid French, all smiles and hand gestures. Finally, he stood, clasped her hand and nodded. Turning to the rest of us, he switched to English. "It was a pleasure meeting you all. I hope we will see more of each other in the next few days."

With a nod and a quick hug for Tulia, he walked off the boat and up the dock.

"Uh," Martin broke the silence eventually. "What just happened?"

"I've agreed to stay in the area for a couple of weeks, to let Tulia have some time with her family. Besides, this is a nice part of the world — it won't hurt us to stay in one spot for a while."

"So we're staying at the docks?" Jimmy asked, a mixture of hope and incredulousness on his face.

"For a day or two," Mat said. "I said we're staying in the area, not that we're swallowing the anchor. So you lot better get your shore leave in now if you want it."

She stalked off down below and the rest of us looked at each other, still a bit confused.

Tulia finally shrugged her shoulders, then grabbed Martin's hand. "It's my life," she said. "I have to do what's right for me, even if it's hard. And I'm not done sailing yet."

"Well, I am," Isaac announced and we all looked at him, aghast. "At least for now. I want my cheeseburger in paradise. Who's with me?"

We all grabbed our going-ashore gear and stepped off the boat. It was so strange to be able to just walk ashore and as we ambled up the dock I turned back to look at the boat. I'd seen boats at docks before, of course, and they'd always looked alternately like toys for the nouveau riche or tools for difficult work. The *Byte Bucket* was different, though. It looked like adventure. It looked like friendship.

   It looked like home.

Acknowledgments

I am deeply grateful to the following people who helped with this book and the entire series:

- ★ Erica L. Satifka, my editor, for her careful and wise comments;
- ★ Amanda Witherell, for convincing me that writing about sailing was cool;
- ★ Dawn Bonanno, S.B. Divya, Elizabeth Shack, and others, for their thoughts on an early draft of *Packet Trade*;
- ★ the Codex writers' group, for too much to mention;
- ★ all the sailors and local people I met on my travels, for sharing their lives and stories;
- ★ and my mate, Steven Ensslen, for everything.

Darusha Wehm is the author of the *Devi Jones' Locker* series and is the editor of the crime and mystery journal *Plan B Magazine*. She is also a published poet.

Writing as M. Darusha Wehm, she is the author of five published science fiction novels, including the award-nominated *Andersson Dexter* cyberpunk mystery series. Her short science fiction has been published in many venues, including *Escape Pod*, *Mothership Zeta* and several anthologies.

She lives in Wellington, New Zealand after sailing down the west coast of the Americas and across the Pacific Ocean with her partner, Steven, on their sailboat, Scream.